ENDURE THE CHAOS

APOCALYPSE FIRE TRILOGY — BOOK ONE

Copyright © 2021 Angry Eagle Publishing, LLC
https://AngryEaglePublishing.com

Cover design by DauntlessCoverDesign.com

Find the author on the web.

Https://AuthoroftheApocalypse.com

Don't forget to sign up for the spam free newsletter

https://bit.ly/3KmAGjh

ENDURE THE CHAOS

APOCALYPSE FIRE TRILOGY — BOOK ONE

DJ COOPER

Other books by DJ Cooper

<u>Dystopia Series</u>
Beginning of the End
Long Road
Revelations
Dark Days

<u>Insurrection Series</u>
Deception
Evasion
Abolition

<u>Nine Meals from Anarchy Series</u>
Sun's Fury
Terminus State

<u>Shadow Wars Series</u>
Invasion
Resistance
Resurgent

<u>Cincinnati Fall Series</u>
Cincinnati Fall

Cincinnati Fall 2

Cincinnati Fall 3

AUTHOR'S NOTE

Many who read post-apocalyptic books note how the characters are all prepared and wonder how characters might do that are not at all prepared. There are stages of grief (and in this case grieving the loss of their world) that most people go through. Developed by Elisabeth Kübler-Ross and published in her book back in 1969 she outlined them as: denial, anger, bargaining, depression, and finally acceptance.

Our characters' actions try to follow how one might view things. How they may not see an issue in the beginning (denial), how they get angry with events and then begin to try and sort through them as though things might go back to normal.

This series will chronicle these stages in our very clueless characters, who will do stupid things and refuse to accept that things are as bad as they are. Read this story through the eyes of the unprepared and see the ways in which you can learn from their mistakes.

ONE

JACE

"Damn dude, this is harsh," Ian coughed.

Sudden vibration beneath them caused small pebbles to dance across the rock. The two shared a wide-eyed glance.

"Did you feel that?" Jace asked, his voice quiet, offering a lopsided smile and passing the joint back to Ian.

Ian laughed and sucked on the small smoldering twist of paper once again, holding the smoke in his lungs before exhaling and again coughing violently. Hoarsely, he choked, "It's only a tremor dude. Chill."

Jace's voice faltered, cracking when he tried to speak, laughing the uneasiness off, determined not to let it bother him. "Pass me another beer will ya? We're celebrating… It's a boy!" he cheered.

Foam rolled over the top when he cracked the lid open and tipped the bottle up. "Ahh…" He smiled and took a long drink. "Hey Ian, did you know aliens may have been the ones who built the pyramids?"

"Jace Walker, you never take anything seriously." Ian scoffed at him.

Jace frowned, his thoughts trailing off elsewhere. The chatter on the dark web kept running through his mind. The company was drilling at some of the fault lines for oil. Claimed it was easier to extract due to the misalignment of the plates. This was a bad idea; he was sure that something was wrong with their process. He managed to get some of the data floating around in mostly unseen places.

When he'd called the assistants to their geologist, they wouldn't listen to him. They were more concerned with how he found out about the project and blew him off trying to appease him with some crap about oil seeping into cracks in the crust. No degree, no job. Damn he needed that job, but the company was looking shady in light of the things he found on the dark web. He needed a decent job and this company up north looked promising. His small family needed this kind of break.

"Pfft. That guy was an idiot. Of course it's a friggin' fault line," Jace blurted.

Ian tilted his head and looked at Jace, his eyebrows pulled together. Jace noted his look and shrugged it off, pretending to be completely wasted and returned to his annoyed thoughts. Some little mama's boy standing over him pontificating, trying to come off as someone important. They'd offered him a position on the rigging crew to appease him, but dammit he knew he could be more useful elsewhere. He shrugged at the icky nagging inside bringing him down. "Hey Ian, you ever been to Utah?"

Ian shrugged, "Naw, man. I need to go though."

"I am thinking of moving to a nice little place and starting over. Maybe even the suburbs. People say there are lots of jobs there. L.A. is the amazing party central, but I gotta think about the kid now, ya know?"

"Uh huh," Ian absently nodded. "I thought you were gonna break up with her," he said, taking a long draw off his beer.

"I was," Jace sighed. "But that was before I found out about the baby. I vowed I would never be like my father if I ever had kids." His voice growing angry, he chugged the last of the beer in his hand. "When he found out my mom was pregnant, he refused to leave his wife and take care of us."

Ian spit his beer out and wiped his chin with his sleeve. "You mean your mom was his side chick? Dude, I didn't know that; my mom was a side chick too."

"Well, I wasn't gonna do that to my boy, he would have a father. I'll admit that this isn't what I had in mind, but I'll take care of him."

"Props dude." Ian held out his fist toward Jace. "My dad bailed, but mom got the bucks from him, so I saw him sometimes and he brought shit."

Again, the ground shook, knocking over the beer. "Damn aftershocks!" Jace scowled. "Waste of a good beer."

He was trying not to sound as freaked as the shaking in his hands would give away.

Ian, originally from L.A., never seemed bothered by the occasional shaking, but it bothered Jace. The tiny quivers under him made his skin crawl as the ground continued to vibrate.

"Hey man, spark up that doobie," Ian quipped, grinning at him. Bright red eyes peeking through slitted eyelids. "We got time before the others come rolling in, let's get wasted."

Ian's head shook and he sprawled out on the massive rock. Jace could tell he was nervous by the way he was creeping as close as he dared. Belly crawling to the edge of their perch that sat high on the side of the mountain.

The view of the city gleamed in the sunshine. It nearly blocked Jace's view of his friend with trembling fingers groping around the boundary of their remote roost over the cliff. Ian found a small slot to grab hold and Jace nearly laughed when the sharp edge pricked his fingertips as he grasped for the crack and wedged them in tight.

Ian sucked a loud breath through his teeth and whistled. "Damn that's a long way down," grinning back toward Jace who was completely satisfied to stay right where he was because he was afraid of heights and would go nowhere near that edge.

Jace gazed out over the city below, the sun reflecting and the red rocks creating a backdrop of crimson sky, shimmering reflections off the Pacific Ocean giving the city a pink aura.

"You know… From here the city looks like a sparkly fantasy kingdom," Jace mused and leaned back against the hillside. His legs stretched out on the giant outcropping, groaning a loud sigh before tilting his face skyward and putting his hands behind his head.

He sniffed the crisp mountain air. "Ahhh, I love it up here, Ian. The air smells fresher, cleaner, you know? The city is smoggy and crowded." Scrunching his nose and then smiling. "I'm gonna take my kid hiking and camping in the fresh air."

Settling into a comfortable spot, relaxing, and letting the warm sunlight soothe him, a calm washed over him, and he dozed.

The ground shook again, harder this time, rocks and dirt from the hillside came rolling down on top of him. A real quake rolled over the hills, not just one of those little tremors from earlier. The swaying motion of the land made the hairs on the back of his neck stand on end as actual fear crept up his spine. He glanced over to his friend, who appeared unfazed, and laughed nervously at him, trying not to look like some jellyfish, Jace joked, "Dude, what a buzz-kill."

Ian laughed and staggered over to piss off the edge of the drop. "Yeah, I hate it when they cluster like this," he complained. "Makes me feel like I'm gonna hurl."

The rumbling began again, and another quake shuddered across the land before the last one had even subsided. This was no small tremor; the shaking grew more intense. Shards of light twinkled from the city in the distance, dancing across the sky as buildings crumpled, sending plumes of dust skyward and leaving the barely visible outlines of twisted steel in their place. L.A. would be in chaos, smoke already rising from the city center, the fairytale kingdom an obliterated wreck.

The hillside began to crumble and Jace lunged for solid ground, crawling toward safety, while narrowly dodging two large rocks rolling his way. A smaller one smashed into his hand before he could move, slamming it hard. Instinctively he jerked the injured appendage away, cradling it to his chest and howling in pain. The rain of rocks continued as he rolled to avoid the deluge. He shimmied left and dodged right trying to stand and run, but the outcropping was already cracking beneath his feet.

He slipped and his foot jammed into the small space between the rocks, twisting his leg unnaturally. Pain from the ankle shot up his leg and he tried to free himself by tugging, but it wouldn't budge. He pulled harder yet it refused to release his foot. The world spun and swayed while Jace panicked. A small tree to his left stretched across his path, he reached out grasping a branch to help him balance. He held it firmly while he struggled and yanked at his foot to free it from the crevasse. Words tried to form in his throat but wouldn't come out. The realization hit him. They could be in real danger.

His whole body buzzed with adrenaline clouding his vision with tears. "Ian, my foot..." he called out. "The rock jammed my leg." He screamed louder to get his friend's attention while furiously tugging in a panic. "Ian, help...I'm stuck!" he yelled at him, grappling with his leg, searching for an out, and scrabbling for balance.

Ian, buzzed and oblivious, stood some feet away from the edge and carried on side stepping while pissing for distance off the side of the rock. Hopping slightly as he pulled up his zipper, he turned to Jace with a smirk, obviously proud of his whizzing prowess. The earth shuddered, hard, and Ian dropped to his belly, clinging to the smooth surface, his hand searching for a place to hold on to.

This slab, dangling over a massive drop, was beginning to pull away.

"Come on." Jace scrambled, clawing at the earth, his foot still wedged tight in the rock. Swiping and scratching at the loose sand, he tried to hoist himself away from the disintegrating hillside, but his foot was still jammed and would not come loose.

"Come on, Ian!" he screamed over his shoulder again. "I don't like the way the rock face is breaking. You need to get over here!"

Ian's rapidly blinking eyes expressed the fear he was experiencing. His face paled with a silent look of resignation, as the rock cracked and tilted further away from the hillside. The pressure on Jace's foot eased, the shift releasing it. Grasping at the small shrubs and dirt, Jace skittered for the safety of the hill, his fears for his friend illuminated by the wide-eyed silent plea for help.

Ian lay frozen on the rock, sprawled out, clinging to a small wedge in the surface. The rock could not hold for much longer. One more shake and the entire ledge would sheer off and plummet. Jace gripped the thorny bush to his right; spikes digging into his palms and held his other hand outstretched to his friend. "Move your ass, Ian! Get up... run, dammit!"

Ian tried to stand, but the rock shifted. Knocked back down, he couldn't stand and scooted toward him with the slab violently shaking beneath. He was making little progress and stumbled, falling to the ground, his hands feverishly clawing at smooth stone.

Jace's heart sank. "Hurry," he pleaded, less forceful and more defeated as the gash between them widened a little more with each quake. It was swiftly becoming obvious his friend would never get across the shaking ground. A loud crack echoed across the canyon and the rock pulled away. His eyes welled up with tears. "NO! Ian-n-n-n-n!".

One last glance from Ian as the ledge slid away. Terror chiseled in his face, grasping at anything within reach in the moments before the massive chunk of rock toppled off the edge. His screams silenced in the crash of rubble below.

Jace, only a few feet from the edge, shuffled backward to move back from the loose earth. His head in his hands, sobbing. His mind spun trying to make sense of what happened. Only moments before they were having fun and relaxing, but now...

"Dammit," he cursed, swiping the wet tracks off his face. "Shit, Kelly..."

Her name hung on the air propelling him forward, limping on his already swollen ankle. His hands shook, blood oozing from the small puncture wounds on his palms. He fished around under a shrub where he stashed a small rucksack earlier to keep it out of the sun. "Please be here," he prayed.

The smooth leather of the small pouch offered some relief from his anxiety, but his fingers refused to heed his instruction and struggled to unlatch the buckle. He reached in and retrieved his cell phone. Fumbling with the lock screen his anxiety grew. Finally dialing her cell, he waited and listened. Three rings and an automated operator voice answered. "All circuits are busy, please try your call again later."

He cursed and punched the dial button again. Same response. His voice growled, "Ugh."

Cramming the phone back into the bag, he reached for the water bottle that sat atop the few meager items he always carried. Dry mouth, a side effect of the weed, made his throat sticky and pasty. Hands shook as he pulled the stopper from the water bottle and squeezed a long stream of the cool liquid into his mouth. It provided a moment of respite and washed away the parched dryness that gave his tongue a sense of being glued to the roof of his mouth.

His head swam from the weed and the adrenaline. As confusion mixed with tears filled his eyes, his heart weighed heavy with guilt over leaving his friend at the bottom of the ravine. He knew there was no way Ian survived and he had to find Kelly.

He produced a couple of band aids to cover the puncture holes, as well as a roll of bright green bandage wrap tape that he wrapped around his ankle. Jace was an avid hiker and felt lucky he'd thought to bring the small pack.

With the water bottle crammed inside, he struggled to his feet. His bloody hand reaching for another limb, he half hopped, and half crawled up the hill to find safety.

Once he reached the narrow path from the lower lot, he found himself trapped; the pathway was gone. A sheer rock face glared at him where the track should have been.

"Crap!" He cursed repeatedly, his head jerking back and forth seeking a way out. He stood on the small ledge staring upward, the only way out now. The climb along the fringe protruding from the hill to the top was steep but not impossible. Fear from the height nearly strangled him as he forced himself to push forward.

"This party sucks," he cursed as he reached for a handhold, a tear rolling down his dirty cheek leaving a path through the dust on his face. He continued to climb the hill one shaky step at a time, while more quakes rocked the area, each immobilizing him. A rock he stepped on gave way beneath his foot and a narrow section fell away; he was frozen in place and clung to a root sticking out of the hill. His muscles screamed as he gripped the shrubbery, terror arresting his ascent at every turn.

He scampered the last few feet to the top and threw himself to the ground landing squarely on the path. In need of a breather, he paused and sprawled out across the red clay soil, grateful for solid ground. His hands held over his face, he lay in a brief moment of retrospection and sobbed.

"What the hell is going on?" he asked no one, sitting up. He had a firm understanding of tectonic plates and fault lines, and though quakes made him nervous, he was sure something else was happening. Recalling what he'd seen about that company doing something with the massive volcano, a ripple of dread ran down his spine.

Two

Cami

A woman's screams echoed down the hallway from the break room. A sound so shrill, the hair on the back of Cami's neck stood up. Her knees shook with fear, but still, she rose to find the source. Her panic subsided as she grew closer and recognized the voice. Her eyes rolled; it was Blythe again.

This was nothing new. Cami recalled one time, when a dust bunny came rolling out from under the fridge and she shrieked so loud the janitor came running to her rescue with a chair held high. Never surprised by her damsel in distress act, she sighed and headed for the doorway. She was fairly sure this was all another stunt, performed with impeccable timing and orchestrated to get the attention of the new office manager.

"He was kind of hot," she smiled and whispered to herself, noting the way he confidently marched through the offices earlier in the day. Cami honestly had no patience for Blythe's antics today. "What now?" She rolled her eyes at the other woman.

"It…It scurried…over there," Blythe said in a panic, pointing to the table.

Cami stood with her back to the other woman making a cup of coffee. Why not? She was in the break room might as well grab a cup of coffee before taking on the giant dust ball. She turned, taking a long sip of her coffee, and crept up on the beast. She nearly snorted the coffee through her nose at the sight of it… It was one ferocious ladybug.

"You mean this?" Cami smirked, holding the small spotted beetle in the air for Blythe to cringe at.

"Yes," she screeched. "Get rid of it!"

"This day can't get any weirder," Cami scoffed, turning to leave with the terrifying bug.

"Why is it so weird?" a husky voice asked.

The voice startled Cami. She spun to see who it was, only to find the new office manager standing in the doorway. A man whom she was now firmly planted directly in front of, nose to chest.

Her voice cracked when she tried to say something, but only a few squeaks emerged.

Meanwhile, Blythe went into a full tirade about the bug that was in the break room and how disgraceful it was.

When she noticed him standing there, she immediately stuck her chest out and slinked on over next to him flinging her long blonde hair behind her shoulder trying just a little too hard to be seductive.

Blythe was a master of the office flirting game. "What brings you to Denver? I hear you're from California; I love San Diego but could never find a job that worked in that economy. Why would you leave?"

Cami rolled her eyes again hearing the rapid-fire questions. A flick of her own hair felt justified, but instead, she silently slid through the doorway glad not to draw the attention of the new boss man.

His name was Theodore James Brandywine the Third. When the head of operations introduced the new manager, he stood stoic, and Cami thought he was stuffy. Too stuffy for a thirty-something that looked as hot as he did. Times sure have changed, this guy had dark hair that fell to his shoulders, and he wore a suit but not a tie. When he spoke, it echoed across the room, yet carried a silky tone. Cami didn't trust him and wanted to remain as unseen as possible. She made her way to her desk snickering at a joke she was hatching to describe the boss man. Something else intrigued her. "But...Wow, he smells good," she smirked, recalling how the scent made her look back at him.

Her escape was fortuitous not to draw attention to herself. She walked along the hallway laughing to herself. He would surely be trapped for the next twenty minutes by Blythe's need for attention. "Theodore James Brandywine the Third," she smirked in a mocking manner while making her way to her desk. "How about Teddy Three?" she muttered and then giggled to herself.

"I like it," the strong and vaguely familiar voice said from behind her. "Why did you leave the breakroom?"

Cami wanted to shrink right into the woodwork. He'd heard her, she was mortified. Up until now her not so flashy, short, plucky, but cute in a plain kind of way demeanor had never been noticed. She'd always blended into the wallpaper next to Blythe, and for him to speak directly to her twice in a matter of minutes meant nothing but disaster.

"Uh, I'm sorry…." she stuttered nervously and shifted her feet. All the while sure she was about to be shown to the door.

Her mind raced and she stood waiting for him to fire her. She mouthed silently to the floor "What the hell Cam, couldn't keep your mouth shut, could ya?"

He laughed, "I've been called worse."

"It's just…um…Well." Cami couldn't think of anything to say to get herself out of this one and stood resolute, sure she'd be looking for a new job this afternoon.

"What's your name?" he asked.

"Cami, I mean, Camilla James," she muttered.

"Nice to meet you Cami," he smiled, then leaned in and whispered so close to her ear she could feel the heat from his breath. "But let's keep the Teddy Three thing between us, shall we?"

Cami felt like fainting, sure she would do just that if he stood there any longer. Her head spun, and she really did feel dizzy. Things looked like they were swaying. He leaned in closer, holding onto the wall behind her. All that hair tousled when he shook his head trying to clear the dizzy feeling he, too, felt. Before they could clear the swimming in their heads the building began to shake violently, knocking them both to the floor. She didn't mean to, but she'd reached out and latched onto him, burying her face into his chest. Terrified, she clung to him while the world around her shook. His strong arm cupped her head and protected her while the other held his jacket over their faces.

All around them people screamed, coffee cups crashed to the floor, and the fluorescent lighting exploded above their heads, raining down small shards of glass throughout the office. The initial shock settled into a low rumbling quake but didn't stop entirely. Theodore rose and helped Cami to her feet, steadying her momentarily.

"I thought I left the earthquakes behind in Cali," he said, brushing the glass from his hair.

"We don't get quakes here." Cami spoke but didn't look at him, her eyes darting about the office, tears welling up.

"We would get them all the time, but this felt different."

"How's that?" she asked, walking on shaky legs beside him.

"In Cali, once it's over, it's over, but this seems to have some kind of continuing rumble."

She looked at him confused. She'd never been in an earthquake and didn't know what to expect. Suddenly she stopped, looking around.

"What's wrong?"

"Where's Blythe?"

"Who?"

"The girl from the breakroom," Cami cried out, nearly in a panic. She hurried through the office area to the place where she'd last seen Blythe and called for her. One of the other women stood by shaking and pointed to a door on the far side of the offices. "She went for a smoke out on the balcony right before the quake."

Cami's eyes widened in horror, and she sprinted for the balcony. They were on the eighth floor and the small balcony never did feel safe to her. When, or more likely if, she ever went out there she clung to the door as if it were the only lifeline from the steep drop to the pavement below. This time was different, she burst through the door to find that there was no balcony. The railing and outside seating area were completely gone. All but a three-foot ledge had broken off on every floor and lay in a pile of rubble on the ground below.

Theodore saw her run through the office in a panic and chased after her. He was right behind her at the door, grabbing the waist of her skirt just in time, jerking her back inside the building. Together they stared out across the devastation, both stunned at the crumbling buildings and smoke rising across the city.

Cami screamed and buried her face into his chest for the second time. He held her close while he leaned over and peered through the doorway. A single look down into the rubble and he sighed. The twisted body of Blythe, half covered in rubble lay broken far below them. Her eyes glazed wide in the last look of terror before she'd crashed into the ground. Her lovely blonde locks now stained crimson with the blood that pooled onto a small slab beside her.

Theodore led Cami inside, where she struggled to regain her composure.

"I'm so sorry," she sniffled, stepping back, and pulling herself together.

"It's ok, we are all a bit freaked right now," he said, putting a hand on her shoulder. "I need to check and see if everyone else is ok. Will you be alright?"

"Yes, I'm good now." She nodded at him, tears rolling freely down her cheeks.

The look in her eyes begged for help even though she'd never ask. Pure terror mixed with sorrow, she felt alone. She was relieved when he reached for her arm. "Come on, Cami. You know everyone here. Walk with me to check on the others."

They both looked around the offices for any other injuries and gathered the small panicked and confused group in the conference room to consider the next steps.

Two people were in the elevator but otherwise safe. It looked like only Blythe had been lost.

Susannah, the receptionist, tried calling 911 several times, but the lines were busy. In fact, all of the lines were busy, the recording repeating the same message, over and over, "All lines are currently busy. Please try your call again later." She tried the emergency line and the non-emergency one as well as a few other numbers looking for her family and got the same message each time.

"I need to get home to my kids," she cried.

"We will all get out of here shortly," Theodore said. "Does anyone know what happened?"

Two guys in the back of the room were chatting animatedly. One of them was getting angry, yelling, "I'm not a conspiracy theorist! Just yesterday the news was talking about it. You should try watching it sometime."

Theodore called out to them, "What was the news talking about?"

The man scoffed at the other man and turned to face everyone. "A company that is fracking all along the San Andreas fault line," he said, confident that his assessment was correct. He threw a side eye glance at the other man before he continued, showing he thought he'd won the argument. "The news was talking about the disturbance kicking off a super volcano or something. Has anyone ever heard of the Dotsero Volcano right here in Colorado? They said it could go off and talked about fracturing the fault system all along the west coast. They mentioned the clustering quakes at Yellowstone last night on the eleven o'clock news."

Cami's eyebrows scrunched together. "A volcano… in Denver? That's ridiculous."

Murmuring and conversation began almost immediately and rose to the level of a roar within seconds.

"What volcano?" Theodore shouted over the increasing volume.

Silence engulfed the room as though he'd said something unmentionable. Cami looked up at him while the man who he'd been arguing with cleared his throat. "You're kidding right?"

Theodore's gaze shifted to Cami. She shrugged, all of it confused her. He glanced around the room at the dozens of eyes before him. Some looked scared, while others seemingly mocked him. "Did I miss some giant volcano in Denver or something?" He shrugged with his hands out palms up.

"Not in Denver, up in the mountains and north in Wyoming, near Montana," the man scoffed. "You know… Yellowstone?"

"This is a joke, right? 'Get the new boss?'" Theodore asked, choking out a nervous laugh. No one else found it funny. He looked at his watch. "It's early yet. There will be no ten o'clock staff meeting. Let's stop for the day and everyone go home. I'm sure there is damage to the building. So, hold off for tomorrow and take a long weekend. We will want to make sure that the building gets checked out." The office staff began milling about and heading for the door when Theodore called out after them, "But plan to be here on Monday."

He waved to each of them and thanked them for helping and muttered to himself, "Great first day. Why not bring an earthquake on day one? That'll make an impression." Cami overheard him but pretended she didn't. She was a little pleased that he was not just some overly confident macho guy.

The murmuring continued as the others went about getting their things to go home. Something was off however, and they knew it. The steady tremor that was like a vibration beneath their feet added credence to the possibility that the man was right. Cami had moved out of the room and sat at her desk organizing some items in her purse for the walk home. Blythe was her ride, and she had a little over twelve miles to walk in order to get home. She hoped the light rail was still running but somehow doubted it.

The firm voice from behind startled her. "Do you think there is something to this volcano?"

"Would you stop doing that?" Cami spun around and snapped.

"Doing what?" Theodore asked.

"Sneaking up on me. Knock it off," she growled at him. She didn't care about the niceties at this point.

"Sorry, I do seem to keep doing that, don't I?" He chuckled then turned to the others lining up to wait for the elevator. "Stairs, people. Take the stairs, the elevator is not safe." Then turned back to Cami, "I wonder if you could help me find the police station. I need to let them know about Blythe and the others in the elevator."

"Sure," Cami sighed.

"You ok?" he asked.

"Yeah," a tear rolled down her cheek, "Blythe was my friend. I know she was a little flaky, but she was really nice. We carpooled together."

The realization stung them both, she was actually dead. "I'm sorry, perhaps I could give you a ride?"

"It's pretty far, like twelve miles. I live in Arvada. It's on the north side of the city."

"That's not a problem, but first we need to go to the police station. Would you mind helping me with her information and the others in the elevators so they can notify someone?"

"Ok," she replied, nodding in gratitude. Shoving her chair aside, she grabbed her purse and jacket and headed for the stairwell. "You got family to check on?" she asked.

"No, it's just me and I must admit I'm a little lost. I only arrived yesterday, and my apartment is still in boxes."

The walk down the stairs had a few obstacles and some debris from the ceilings, but they were able to make it to the first floor. When they emerged from the building, some of the rubble from the balcony lay piled up beside the door. And Blythe lay just beyond, her body twisted and broken, eyes staring skyward. Theodore took his coat off and laid it over her face before they climbed into his BMW and headed out. The roads had some collisions and debris, but the car easily skirted these.

They arrived at the police station, and it was buzzing inside with activity. Bits and pieces of information could be overheard while they stood filling out paperwork for the incident.

"A person is dead, and we are standing here filling out paperwork," Cami complained loudly.

"I imagine there are more people dead," Theodore said, his voice calm and steady.

"Probably," Cami conceded. "But I didn't know them."

"I'm more worried about the people in the elevator."

Cami hung her head, slightly embarrassed. "I'm sorry, yes, their situation is far more urgent."

He put his hand on her shoulder and gave her a half smile. Before another word was spoken, a thunderous roar filled their ears, and the station shook as another quake rocked the earth beneath their feet. He grabbed her arm and dragged her out the door, racing from the station into the open. A man outside stared off to their left; his mouth hung wide as though he'd speak but without any words. They followed his gaze and saw the black curtain slowly advancing over the mountains in the distance of the western sky.

THREE

JACE

L.A. was burning, the once glamourous city was now a crumbling mass of destruction, illuminated by only the sullen orange glow.

Jace's girlfriend, Kelly, was down there. Her boss had called her in to work to cover for a colleague. "Only for a couple of hours." He glanced at his watch. She should have made it home by now. Maybe? He needed to find her, wherever she was.

His ankle throbbed and stung, and he needed some support if he was going to head down this mountain to find her. A branch from the wreckage of trees looked like a good cane. A quick strip of the twigs and leaves made a workable but rough walking stick.

A loud snap behind him sent him spinning. His nerves on edge, the muscles in his forearms tensed, and his grip tightened around the stick. He held the limb out before him in defense ready to strike.

The whimper caught him off guard and he relaxed

his stance. A massive Rottweiler stood before him, tongue hanging out and front paw up. Jace took a step toward the dog, and a low rumble welled up within its throat. Cowering briefly before limping forward. The dog yelped and stopped, paw dangling.

Jace put his hand out for the dog to sniff, but the animal growled, pulling back. Jace tried to skirt around the dog but couldn't squeeze past on the narrow path. Mustering all his courage and digging deep, he lowered the stick and crouched, his hand out palm down, trying to appear submissive. The dog sniffed at him briefly and sat. Jace's shoulders slumped in relief and he shook his head. "Ok then, please don't eat me," he whispered.

Daring to inch a little closer, Jace reached out and scratched the animal behind the ear. He liked animals better than people most days and felt sure the poor dog needed help. His hand followed the soft fur down the shoulder to the paw. The dog jerked away, snapping at him, almost catching his hand.

"C'mon..." he cooed and looked under the animal noting it was a boy. "C'mon boy, let's have a look at that paw."

He inched closer to the dog for a peek at the underside of the paw without touching the dog's injury. Jace winced when he spotted the top from a glass bottle embedded in his paw. He leaned back on his heels. "I don't have time for this."

The sides of his mouth raised in a crooked smirk at

the dog, trying to hide his terror. He cooed at the animal, "Ok buddy, this is gonna hurt."

He briefly checked the glass in the paw then the muzzle of the huge dog. His tongue was hanging out exposing his massive white canines. "And... ahh... Don't bite me, ok?"

In a single swift motion, Jace snatched the glass out of his paw while dancing backward out of the reach of his substantial jaws. The dog yelped, growling, and snapping. He cast Jace a pained look and flopped down to lick the bloody gash. Jace hurried to his pack for something to wrap the wound and returned with a roll of gauze and a slab of jerky. He offered the jerky to the dog, who sniffed and carefully took it from Jace's hand.

Jace raised his eyebrows at the gentle nature of the Rottweiler. "You aren't so scary now, are you?" He scratched under the dog's chin. The dog accepted it hesitantly. He was too occupied with his now profusely bleeding paw to object.

Jace sat down to wrap the paw, keeping the dog sidetracked with another piece of jerky. Jace secured it with more of the green tape to ensure the dog didn't rip the bandage off. At least until the bleeding stopped.

Another tremor and Jace fell to the ground gripping the frightened dog. The shaking stopped almost as quickly as it had begun. He stood and shook his head, trying to shake off the uneasy feeling the quake had left behind.

Jace kissed the air a couple times, looking at the dog,

"C'mon boy, let's get off this rock before there are any more." Slapping his leg, he encouraged the dog to follow. "Now," he looked around. "Where's your master?"

The dog whimpered, but limped along, trying to keep up. Jace was hobbling as fast as he could on his crooked stick. A trail of drying red droplets left by the dog's bloody paw left a trail to follow down the small foot trail. When they reached the lower section, he found the reason the dog was wandering the hills alone. They both stared at the motionless body of his master. The dog crept up beside the lifeless body, whined and licked the now graying hand.

A huge boulder had crushed the young hiker. Blood and brain matter oozed from his smashed skull, barely visible beneath the enormous mass of red sandstone. The sight of it made Jace gag, he had to look away to keep from throwing up.

The hiker had a small pack and a real walking stick. Jace grimaced but still gathered them from the body. He also took the hiker's wallet, figuring it would help police once they got to the city to identify him. Jace planned to return the other items as well once they reached the police station. Further searching revealed a leash and collar. Jace picked it up and shook it at the dog, "I assume this is yours?"

The frightened animal with his big brown eyes acknowledged it. "Humph."

At the end of the leash, the round collar hung, still buckled. "Squeezed out of this, did you?" Jace offered a strained smile, dangling it, the tags jingling together. He spied a small dog bone with the name Boon embossed.

"Boon? Is that your name?"

The dog's ears perked up. "Let's go, Boon, Ian's car is down the hill, we need to skedaddle out of here."

Jace put the collar on the dog and tugged on the leash, but the dog didn't want to leave his master. He coaxed Boon with another piece of jerky, and the two set off down the gravel road to the lower lot. His thoughts kept circling from Kelly to the quakes, trying to make sense of what happened, his worry for her rising to almost a panic.

The dog sniffed at his hand in search of another piece of jerky. Jace absentmindedly wiped the steamy hot breath onto his pants. His eyes widened, and he shot a glance at the dog, then up across the expanse of the city, and back to the dog. He finally figured out what bothered him about the way the quakes felt and why they were so different.

"Boon! You're a genius. C'mon."

Ian's car sat exactly where they'd left it. Jace's shoulders sank in relief while a twinge of sadness washed over him. He knew Ian was dead but they approached the vehicle cautiously, as if he were a thief stealing the car. Boon sat while Jace climbed under the rear bumper, then shimmied to the side of the car, jamming his arm up inside the wheel well in search of the hide-a-key.

"I know it's here," Jace grunted, reaching further back. "Found it." He smiled at the dog. Satisfied, he scooted forward from under the car, key in hand.

Quakes rocked the area again. Rocks rained down upon them, throwing Jace off balance, and slamming him into the side of the car. Grappling, he tried to get out of the way of a large boulder rolling down the hillside toward him.

SMASH!

It slammed into the rear panel of the car. "Ahh." Jace's scream echoed through the canyons. He was now pinned between the car and boulder. He gritted his teeth and grunted, using his legs to shove the boulder that held his arm wedged. It didn't budge the first try, but he kept trying, shifting his position to get more leverage. He rocked it until finally... it moved. A tiny bit of movement was enough to wriggle his arm loose and he was free.

Hopping from behind the car and scurrying around it, he called out, "Boon, buddy... where are you?" Craning his head to listen, Jace limped toward the sound of Boon growling. "C'mon boy." Lips pursed, he whistled for the dog. The shrill screech echoed and bounced off the canyon walls and right back to his ears.

He paused and listened again. Another sound mixed with the dog's barks that made the hairs on the back of his neck raise as the shiver crawled over him. He skipped and hobbled in a hurry to find him. Rounding the corner of the small hill jutting out on the far side of the lot, he came to an abrupt halt and gasped. A large mountain lion hissed, facing off with Boon.

"Hey, you..." Jace shouted with his arms up to look intimidating, waving the walking stick in the air. "Shoo."

The cat roared and lunged at Jace, knocking him down in a pass before turning to face off with him. Boon leaped at the giant cat rolling him over and away from Jace.

Jace jabbed at the cat with the walking stick. It lashed out and swatted the stick away with its massive paw. Boon bit hard on its hind haunch, and the cat roared, slashing with his razor-sharp claws. Another bite from Boon's powerful jaws and the cat ran up over the hill with Boon in close pursuit. Jace called, but the dog snarled and drooled, nipping at the cat's long tail.

Limping after them, Jace stopped short when Boon yelped loudly. His heart raced and pace quickened. "Oh my God... Boon!" He whistled but heard nothing... Again, he whistled. Anxious growling and barking led the way and Jace followed the sounds. Climbing over a small hill he saw them, his heart leapt into his throat overjoyed that the dog was ok. Roars resounded across the hills, while Boon danced beneath a large tree where he'd stranded the snarling animal. He circled the tree, growling, yelping, and jumping.

Jace let out an exaggerated sigh. "Boon... C'mon boy."

The dog limped over to him nudging his snout into Jace's palm. The cat jumped from the tree and hightailed it into the hills. Jace rubbed Boon's head and checked him for injuries. It was difficult to see because his head swiveled side to side, watching for the return of the cat. He'd run the animal off and had a few more scratches to add to his paw injury, but otherwise seemed fine as he pranced proudly alongside Jace to the car.

Key in hand, Jace pressed the unlock button and opened the door. Boon readily hopped into the passenger seat. Jace chuckled at him while casting an uneasy glance over his shoulder. He cursed when he bumped his ankle climbing into the driver's seat. The cat had scared him, and he quickly slammed the door, for fear it would reemerge. Shoving the key into the ignition, he murmured to Boon without looking at him. "Not sure how Kelly will feel about you, but let's go get her. I'm sure that once I tell her how you just saved my life, she'll love you. We're a team now, right?"

The car started without an issue and Jace hoped it had enough umph to escape the large rock pressed firmly against the rear passenger door. At this point he wasn't worried about damage to the vehicle, he just wanted to get out of there. He reached out and scratched under the dog's chin, grabbed the steering wheel, and mashed the gas pedal. Pebbles clattered, plinking on the rear panels of the car when they shot out from behind the tires. A loud squeal made him cringe as the boulder scraped along the side of the car. Once they were clear of it, he could see the boulder roll in the rear-view mirror, into the next car.

A shiver shuddered through him. He could easily have been killed if the rock had hit him full on. Navigating the dirt road to the street below was slow, weaving around the fallen rocks and trees, but they made the mile and a half down the hill without incident.

Once they reached the pavement, he noticed the houses along the drive were still standing with only minor damage. Jace wondered optimistically if the quake only felt worse because of the mountains. He envisioned Kelly safe at the house and found himself renewed, eager to get to her. He hoped she was already home when the quakes began. Silently reasoning with himself to avoid thinking the worst. "It is closer, and her meds were there. Not that she ever left home without them." He turned to Boon who looked back at him with perked up ears. "It's all going to turn out fine." His grip on the wheel tightened and he turned onto the roadway toward home.

On his way down into the city, cars were scattered off the road on the narrow stretch along the hillside. He could see at least one car that lay at the bottom of a steep drop off. A crowd of onlookers peered over the edge; the ripped guardrail dangled, bouncing in the air. Boon's head hung partially out the window, sniffing in the breeze, and inspecting their surroundings.

"I know boy, I smell it too." The acrid odor of burning rubber mixed with the oaky smell of wood stung their eyes the closer they got to home. "Wait till we get there."

He slammed on the brakes. Boon fell to the floorboard.

The disoriented dog grunted, "Rumph."

"Sorry." Jace winced at him. His hands pounded the steering wheel. The bridge over the wash was gone, a pile of rubble in the dry creek bed below. A glance ahead showed smoke rising in the direction of his neighborhood. He rammed the car into reverse and swung it around into a driveway, knocking Boon into the door. The tires chirped when he dropped it down into drive and raced back up the hill.

"You ok, buddy?" He petted the dog, who looked at him suspiciously, leaning against the back of the seat.

"Did you see the smoke and collapsed houses over there? What am I going to do? It's a good four miles to get around the bridge." Boon turned to look back out the window as though he understood. Jace raced through the small streets. "I gotta get there." His voice shook, he wasn't feeling as confident as he was a few moments ago. "She needs me. I have to be there for the baby!"

Roads narrowed, all the while, increased debris cluttered their path. The downward stares of nameless faces drilled into Jace from the small gathering of people. As he passed by, they looked to him, emanating fear in their hollow eyes, sitting hopeless in front of a collapsed house. Some were injured, their bloody clothing tattered and dirty, but he could not stop to help them. Kelly needed him and it had already been too long.

Jace braced Boon against the seat, mashing the brake pedal hard. The car skidded on the dust and rubble before stopping. An entire apartment building lay across the road.

"Crap!"

He spun the car around and took a small side road to get around it. More and more debris littered his path. His house was a mere four miles away, but still out of reach. Another side street, a circle around the block, and it too was closed. A crash blocked the road. The car's engine idled as he stared at it, anger welling up. 'Just do it.' He gauged the distance between the crash and the apartment building.

'Do it!' His inner voice screamed. Jace gripped the steering wheel tighter, flooring the accelerator. The car jerked and rocked when he hit the curb and bounced onto the sidewalk. A screech of tortured metal pierced his ears as the car ripped free of the entangled cars, scraping along the building.

An aftershock rocked the area at the same time. Small bricks fell, shattering the passenger side of the windshield, cracks spidering into view. He pressed the pedal harder trying to push through, thumping over everything in his path, but yet unable to get the rest of the way through.

The rear window imploded, showering both of them with glass. Boon yelped and cowered in the seat. "What the...?" Jace looked over his shoulder to see a young man's body lying across the trunk of the car. His head, dangling through the back window, stared at him from the back seat. A trickle of blood oozed from between his lips. Jace gasped in horror and jumped from the vehicle, stepping back a few feet, shocked, staring at the car.

A skyward glance to find where the man had come

from revealed a shattered window on the fourth floor. Suddenly aware of the reality of the body on the vehicle, he tried to open the door, but the massive dent in the roof jammed the door shut. Jace hesitantly reached through the rear window to feel for a pulse. The man was dead.

He shuddered at the sight and cast a worried glance at Boon, shaking his head. He stepped back but the curve of twisted metal and glass scraped the underside of his forearm when he pulled his arm through the broken window. Blood oozed in an instant from beneath his shirt and he hissed a breath across his teeth, wincing in pain.

"Seriously?" He cursed, grasping at the long gash. His pack had a few first aid supplies but nothing to stitch it up… if he could even do it with his left hand. He reached into the front seat, grabbed his pack, and pulled out a bandage and two band aids. He used them to tug the wound shut, covered it with gauze and secured the whole thing with the green tape.

"This will have to do." Jace winced when he moved the arm.

He pulled the leash from the pack and clipped it to Boon. "Let's go, Buddy."

They headed down the street limping in the direction of his home. He was determined to reach Kelly.

"Only four miles to go."

Four

Cami

They could see a fine, fluttering, gray snow softly landing on the cars. Each of them neatly parked in rows across the meticulously lined blacktop. The month is August and there shouldn't be snow. Not yet, it's too soon for that. The ominous black curtain obscured the warming rays of the sun and a chill shuddered over her that confirmed their fears.

Fears about the small snippets of news the man said predicted this scenario. Cami vaguely recalled highlights nestled in a short bulletin between the dealings of governmental issues and who won the Academy Awards last year. An occasional note about quakes or something called uplift around known volcanoes made news in the past few weeks, but nothing could have prepared them for this.

A frightening scene playing out before their eyes; the Yellowstone super eruption could be happening, and they had front row tickets.

"C'mon, Cami. We need to go."

"But," she objected.

"They have all they need. Let's get you home."

She nodded and followed him to his car. A single streak ran down her cheek. The path of a tear in the gray dust that covered her face.

He paused and turned to look at her. "Do you know how to get to Bloomfield, from Arvada?"

"You mean Broomfield?"

He shrugged and said, "Told you I'd only been here a day."

She smirked at him, "Yes, I do, it's not far from me. First, I agree with you, we gotta get out of this area, these buildings look like they are ready to crumple at any moment."

He glanced around, his eyes darting from one building to another before opening the passenger door for her. She smiled at him and climbed in. In no time they were headed out of town, her directing him as they went. Shifting directions multiple times to avoid accidents or debris in their way.

She pointed to an onramp. "Go left here. Let's get on I-70 and go west. Hopefully, it will be better."

They rode along in silence watching crumpled buildings and fires burning on either side of the highway, but the overpasses seemed to be intact except for one. The whole eastbound side was gone. They raced across the overpass going west, silently gritting their teeth. Once on the other side they both sighed, glancing at one another in relief.

"Another couple of exits and you'll want to take Wadsworth."

Theodore nodded to her without looking and continued to dodge debris and cars stopped in the road. As she'd said, the exit sign appeared.

"Two more miles." He chanced a glance at her.

She watched out the window and grunted back at him, lost in the scene before them. He tilted his head, his eyebrow raised. She was grateful for the ride but felt awkward around him. His expression shifted as though he couldn't decide if he was fascinated or irritated.

With only a mile to go, he mashed the brakes, screeching the car to a halt, slamming Cami into the dash. "Ow!" She yelped.

A pileup of cars blocked the entire road. They peered into the wreckage and spotted injured people standing off to the side. He put the car in park to see if they could help but before they'd managed to get out, another car careened into the back of them. The impact spinning them, lurching it forward, and slamming them back into their seats.

The rear of the car spun and slammed into another. Cami cried out again when her head smashed into the side window. Theodore reached for her, turning her face toward his. A small trickle of blood had already begun to roll down her forehead, stopping at her brow and shifting down her cheek. Frantically, he searched the car for something to cover the injury. With no supplies in the rented car, he tore off the bottom of his shirt, wadding it up and placing it on her head where she'd hit the glass.

He looked at her intently. "Are you ok?"

"I think so," she winced.

"What's my name?"

"Teddy Three," she giggled and winced again, reaching for her head.

He smiled. "You're ok."

Her side of the car was smashed and climbing out of the driver's side turned out to be a struggle. He exited and reached in for her. She flung her bag and jacket out at him and crawled over the console in the center of the car nearly falling headfirst out of the driver's seat.

His swift movement offered a view of his muscular arms when he reached out, catching her before she fell.

He righted her but lingered a bit longer than would have been expected. She looked up at him and he stepped back stammering for words. "I'm ah… Good thing you didn't… I mean."

"A girl could get used to this."

"Wha?" He looked at her, eyebrows raised in question.

"Relax there Superman. I was just teasing. You seem to keep saving me is all," she said brushing away imaginary wrinkles in her skirt.

"Oh." He laughed with an awkward hesitation.

"I didn't mean…"

He waved his hand. "I know, I know. It's just that," he hesitated, "I have no clue where we are. That, and I am not used to having someone, let alone a girl, tell me what to do. I'm feeling a little out of my element."

Cami put her hands on her hips and her eyebrows furrowed, a dark cloud crossed her face. "A girl?"

He wasn't listening to her. He hurried into the back seat of the car, grabbed his bag and hoisted it to his shoulder. Handing her the bag and jacket she'd tossed out of the car, he urged her to go.

Practically dragging her, they hurried to the side and up the road until he could take a moment in the grassy median. Bent over, his hands on his knees, he searched the grass with his eyes.

"What was the rush?" Cami asked, kneeling on the grass beside him. "Shouldn't we have stayed at the scene?"

"I'll just call a tow later. I just felt the need to get out of there."

"I can understand that. A lot actually, I feel that way all the time," she quipped, poking at the wound on her head and wincing.

"Let's go," he said, holding out his hand to help her up. She grasped it and rose, but the ground shook again knocking her back to her knees. The sounds around them were loud and grating. Car metal grinding against one another and the pavement. Screams followed by instant silence. Cut off by the finality of the collapsed overpass.

Once the shaking stopped, the two of them looked down where the rubble from the bridge and cars sat in a mangled twist of metal and cement. The car at the bottom with a large chunk of the roadway deck crushing the seats and trunk. Bodies of those who'd been on the bridge when the quake hit were strewn and bloody below. Cami turned and retched, sobbing.

Theodore hurried over to her and touched her back. She stood and choked a bit more, spitting into the grass and wiping her mouth on her sleeve. He looked at the silky shine of her ponytail and reached for a touch, accidentally catching some on his watch.

She spun around and saw her hair tangled in the band and rolled her eyes grasping for it to untangle it. The length of her hair was often an irritation; she pulled the small elastic tie from it and let her auburn tresses fall around her shoulders. The long locks fell past her waist with a few stray strands across her face that she gingerly tried to wrangle without making her head bleed again. He stood there aghast, his mouth open, as though a word was stuck and wouldn't emerge.

"What?" she asked.

"What?" He looked at her, innocently blinking. "Oh, nothing. I didn't realize you had so much..." He paused. "Hair."

"Hair?" She laughed, "yeah it grows fast." She absently reached up and grabbed it gathering it to the side and wove it into a long braid that hung down her slender figure. Then she tied her jacket around her waist and slung her bag across her body looking at him expectantly. "Well?"

"Ok, yes," he stammered. Slinging his bag over his shoulder he looked around for a sign then back to Cami. "Which way?"

"Well unfortunately, we ran in the wrong direction and will need to get to the other side."

The fence was high, but a small section had a break that they squeezed through. The area on the other side was a pond and marsh. The ground was squishy, and Cami lost her low heel in the gooey mud. Theodore retrieved it but she walked the rest of the way through the ick in her bare feet. Leaping a few times when it felt a little too icky, she danced lightly four or five steps before they made it to the side of the pond. On a bench she sat rinsing the mud off her feet. Once she put her shoes back on the sneer erased from her face.

"We aren't too far," she said. "Won't take more than an hour to get there."

Theodore looked at the unfamiliar territory as they walked, an uneasiness in his gait. Cami strode along confidently, occasionally pausing to wait for him to catch up. He was so busy watching her walk, he plowed right into a bike, hoisted up and chained next to a light pole.

Cami came running, "Are you ok?"

"Yeah, I was watching the street names," he lied. "I am not sure where we are, but I am sure I will be just as lost after we get you home."

She smiled at him. "Not to worry. I'm sure Dad will let me use his Jeep when we get there."

Cami stole a glance at him while they were walking. The wide-eyed fascination with everything around them reminded her how lost he must feel. She thought about how he'd tried to save her at every turn, even in the break room after Blythe had tried her best to get his attention. A sly half smile crossed her lips before her heel caught and she toppled over a crack in the sidewalk, falling to the ground.

He hurried over to help her up. "Are you ok?"

She brushed herself off trying to look injured. Following a play right out of Blythe's bag of tricks she'd seen all too often, she stepped forward and cried out.

"Oww!"

"What's wrong?" His arm sliding around her waist to hold her up.

She smiled slightly before looking up at him. "I ... I must have twisted it," she lied.

She'd nearly forgotten about the ground rumbling, while playing this cat and mouse game, and he'd found himself happily holding his arm around her waist. Until the shaking became violent again. Bricks toppled down around them from the buildings. They hurried to climb into a bus stop shelter to keep the falling debris from hitting them.

Cami twirled her ankle around, saying, "I think it's better, we might want to hurry and get to my house. It's the next block over, right around this corner."

"Are you sure?"

"Yeah…I think it is ok." She knew there was never anything wrong with it but limped slightly anyway as they half jogged, half fast walked to her house.

The ash had begun to fall again and this time it was much heavier. Reaching her house in only a few minutes, she ran up the steps and shoved the large red door open slamming it into the wall. They shook the ash off and brushed it from their clothes on the porch, Theodore reached out and brushed a small bit from the back of her head. A curious shiver teased her senses, her eyes turning to meet his before she ran into the house. Theodore was right behind her cautiously looking about the house as he stepped through the entry.

Cami hurried through the house calling out, "Dad…Dad, where are you?" She cast a glance backward to Theodore and shrugged. "Joey? Anyone? C'mon guys, anyone here?"

Moments later a large man emerged from the basement steps carrying a roll of plastic and some duct tape. "Cami? Is that you?"

"Yeah Dad, where's Joey?"

"He's coming," he said and looked to Theodore. "Who's this?"

"Sorry Dad, this is Theodore Brandywine; he's my boss."

He stuck his hand out immediately. "Sir. My friends call me Theo."

"Don't call me sir, son," he said, grasping his hand firmly and shaking. "Douglas James. Er…Just Doug. How did you come to bring Cami home?"

"Dad, it was awful. Blythe was on the balcony when the first quake hit, and it collapsed." She began to cry, and Theodore reached for her.

Her father's right eyebrow went up observing the moment with a suspicious squint. "And how is it that he came to bring you home?" His voice emphasizing the *he*.

"We had to go to the police station to report some people stuck in the elevator and…" She sniffed. "And Blythe."

"Sorry sir, I'm afraid I only just arrived in Denver. It was actually my first day. I had no idea where the police station was. Cami here offered to go with me to give them all the information about her friend."

Her father relaxed and gave Theodore a once over, looking him up and down, then went to Cami who was blowing her nose on a paper towel.

"I'm sorry about Blythe, honey."

"I was going to have to walk home from work, but Theodore offered to bring me. Then his car got smashed on the highway." She turned her head and lifted her hair wincing. "Look."

Dried blood on her forehead was hidden by her thick hair. Pieces clung to the area and stuck to her head. Her father grabbed for one of the paper towels, wetting it, and flashed Theodore an angry look before dabbing at the area.

Cami shoved the soggy wad away. "Dad, I'm fine. But now we need to help Theodore get home. Can I use the Jeep?"

"I live in Bloomfield."

Her father gave him a quizzical look with a furrowed brow. "Bloomfield?"

Cami giggled. "He said he's only just arrived. "Broomfield."

"Yes, that's right. Broomfield."

He nodded in understanding. "That's pretty close. Where in Brrrr-oomfield do you live?"

"Daaaaad, knock it off."

Arm high she waved to Theodore to follow her into the attached garage. She hopped into the vehicle and started the jeep, motioning him to get into the passenger seat.

FIVE

JACE

Smoke blanketed the area and Jace scrunched his nose recognizing the noxious smell, it was undeniable, its tangy acidic scent laced with carbon and sulfur. The acrid taste in Jace's mouth could only be… rubber. His throat burned from the poisonous gasses and his ankle screamed in pain, but he limped on. Boon whined and crept lower to the ground to avoid the asphyxiating smoke.

They rounded a corner getting closer to the source. A jolt stung his eyes when he saw it. The sight was ominous, the spiraling black cloud mingled with an orange glow and extreme heat. All of it emanating from the Tire Depot. The building, fully engulfed and burning out of control tore at his heart with worry for Kelly and the baby. She was alone in this chaos and every turn held a new obstacle.

A gust of wind whipped his shoulder length hair around, stinging when it furiously slapped his face. The wind changed and the smoke blew in the opposite direction and for a moment breathing was easy. Gulping in the clean air he bent over momentarily with his hands on his knees gasping and coughing to expel the fetid fumes. Hair stuck to his face in the wet streaks of tears that ran freely from his burning eyes. He ran his fingers through the top of his hair and tied that section with a thin hair tie that he pulled from his wrist. The simple act of strangling the unruly mass into the pony and out of his face helped him take in the full scene.

From inside his pocket, he retrieved his cell phone and searched for a signal. "Nothing! I knew better than to go with a prepaid." Shoving the useless item back into his pocket he reached for Boon's leash. "We've got to find Kelly. She'd better be at home where she can get to her meds. Let's go."

Walking on his swollen ankle became increasingly more difficult with the pain shooting up his leg. He'd never make it this way, at least not in time to make sure she had her insulin. Hurried hop-walking succeeded in a push to move away from the suffocating smoke. The dead hiker's stick was not offering much support and he was tiring quickly.

He needed something else, something stronger. About halfway up the block. Shattered glass lay strewn in front of a grocery store. As he drew closer, two people paced outside confused and battered. One pressed a button on her key fob over and over causing the car five or six spaces up to chirp. An old gentleman sat on the bench to the right of the entrance. Jace approached him cautiously, clearing his throat to gain his attention. "Excuse me. Do you know if the store is open?"

The man's gaze remained stoic and unchanged, as though he never heard him. Jace cleared his throat again loudly and touched the man's arm. "I was hoping to find some sports tape and perhaps a cane or crutch here, do you know if it's open?"

The man shook his head, his hands quivered, and tears welled up in his eyes. "They're dead." He rocked, his head hung, with a small bag clutched close to his chest.

Jace took a step back, blinking rapidly processing the information. "Sir... Sir." He knelt in front of the old man. "Sir, what happened? Who's dead?"

The man's hollow eyes were haunting. The hair on the back of Jace's neck prickled. Run home, it warned. Save Kelly and the baby; keep them safe from this madness.

The man spoke again. "My Maria," his voice hitched. "She was…" His mouth opened, but no sound emerged, the horror stuck in his throat. His face wretched in pain he sputtered. "The shelves."

An image formed of the event. The man's few words and momentary gaze indicated something inside the store. Jace placed his hand on the old man's shoulder comforting him. "If you don't mind holding him," holding out Boon's leash. "I'll go check." The man's head bobbed up and down slowly while he reached out for the nylon tether to the dog. He handed the old man Boon's leash, leaned the hiker's walking stick against the bench, and slid off the backpack. Momentarily he thought about leaving his own satchel but instead simply shifted the weight of it, turning for the door to peer inside. Boon whimpered and barked but Jace put his hand up motioning him to stay.

Glass littered the floor and he carefully stepped over large chunks from broken bottles. His sandals barely provided protection from the debris, and he would need to be careful or a twisted ankle would be the least of his worries. He squinted into the darkened store where the only light filtered in from the broken window up front. A sticky liquid oozed across the floor, and he slipped. Reaching for a loose cart to save himself, his arm slammed into the handle, landing squarely on his injury from the car. He wasn't sure where the gooey liquid was coming from and wasn't particularly interested in finding out. He stepped around the section of shelving tipped over in front of him and called out into the darkness. "Maria?" There was no response.

He continued cautiously into the store. Reflections that lingered too long or items crashing to the floor made him jumpy. In the pharmacy section he found a bottle of Motrin and recalled the reason he'd come. The darkness raised the hair on his neck as though an unseen foe were right behind him. He spun around searching the darkness but saw no one. "Screw this... I'm outta here." A single crutch lay beside the blood pressure machine. He picked it up, tucking it under his arm. "This'll do." Grabbing two rolls of the sports tape from the shelf next to it, he hurried to the exit.

At the front of the store, the checkout sat empty. He paused and considered the items in his hand, then the register. He scrawled a hasty note with the items he took along with his phone number noting the emergency need. With some tape from the drawer, he attached the small note to the lane light, and turned for the door.

A voice behind him sneered, "Are you going to steal those?"

Behind him emerged a small man, balding, with a blue apron, with a name tag squarely affixed to the front. Jace squinted to read the tag, "Steve? Is that your name? I left a note with my phone number." Yanking the note from the light he handed it to him. "I only have a credit card and there is no power."

"So, you just steal things?" The man jerked the paper from Jace glancing at it, then peering suspiciously at him through squinted eyes

"No... I wasn't stealing them. No one is here to run the card even if the power was on."

The man was unmoved and Jace fished around in his pockets for any money. "Here," he stretched out his hand with a few crumpled dollars and some coins. "This is all I have. We can figure out the rest later." His eyebrows raised hopeful.

"What's in the bag?" His head bobbed, nosing at the pack Jace carried. "Do you have more stuff in there you aren't mentioning that you're steeeealing?"

"This?" Jace reached for his satchel, lifting the bag, and opening the flap. "Nothing of value, a few pieces of jerky, a couple of snacks, my journal, and a water bottle."

"How about that small box?" The man craned his neck to see what the small pack held. "Did you steal that too?"

Jace was becoming irritated with the little man, ripped the flap back over the pack. "That's it, I'm done." Ignoring his objections, he turned to walk away before things escalated further. His hand reached out and snatched a pack of lighters, waving them in the little man's face. "Add these to the list."

He had to get to Kelly, and he needed the crutch. His pace quickened as he limped toward the door with the little man on his heels. The man grabbed at the crutch and Jace snatched it back, shoving him to the floor. He tried to scramble to his feet, but Jace pressed him down with the crutch to his chest. "Listen Mr. Cashier Man, I'll come back after everything settles down but for now...Back off!"

Steve the cashier rummaged around in his pockets and pulled out his cell phone. His nostrils flared. "I'm calling the police."

"Go for it." Jace's lips curled, and his eyes narrowed.

"I haven't been able to find a signal since this all started." He shot an angry glance at Steve before he stepped through the broken frame of the window.

Boon spotted Jace as he emerged and bolted from the man's grip. The hollow-eyed old man remained in the exact same spot, muttering "Maria" over and over. He sat exactly as he'd left him. Even now, unmoved, staring at the ground, oblivious that Boon had escaped.

He wished he could do more for the man but he couldn't help him and hurried with Boon on his heels across the parking lot. On the next block, he spotted a bus enclosure with a bench. "Come on, Boon." He hopped on the crutch to the seat inside and paused to rest. He lifted the foot to lay across his leg and chanced a view of the substance he'd slipped on. Smeared across his sandal and his toes. A red sheen... Blood.

Bile roiled in his throat, and he gagged. Swallowing hard he pulled the water bottle out of his pack and used a little to rinse it off, winding the tape to get a tighter wrap around his ankle, it felt sturdier.

He needed a few minutes to rest and offered Boon another piece of jerky while he snacked on a few crackers to settle his stomach. There was nothing he could do, he shook his head and shoved four Motrin into his mouth. Followed by what was left in the near empty water bottle to wash them down.

He rested and his mind wandered, going back to the hillside and Ian. Tears welled up, stinging his eyes, while he examined the devastation. His eyes tracing the damage before him, like a bad movie, the events of the past few hours played out.

"You know Boon... I sure wish I had a doobie." He scratched the dog behind the ear. "We always had good smoke. But...I promised Kelly this little soiree was the last time. I was going to quit. Ian..." His voice failed him. "Dammit Ian, why didn't you listen?" He swiped at the tear that had rolled down his cheek and balled up his fist, slamming it into his knee.

Pain shot up his leg from the injured ankle and he grimaced, gripping the bench as though it would somehow stop the agony. Once it passed, his hand fished beneath the bench, searching. The stick was not there. He slapped his forehead. The hiker's pack and the walking stick; they were still on the bench next to the old man back at the store. He'd forgotten them. When Boon came running, he didn't return to the old man. He cursed under his breath, "How stupid."

He muttered while gathering the other items. "Only a block away." There was not much inside, but it did have a few useful items. He shoved the empty water bottle back into his satchel and stood. "C'mon we need to go back."

With the crutch he could move faster, and they hurried back to the store. He halted at the corner and scurried backward, jerking Boon's leash harder than he'd intended. A group of gang members surrounded the store clerk in the parking lot. Tattooed arms swung, lashing at him with fists as they shoved the man around the circle. The old man still sat in the same place while another two rummaged through the hiker pack.

He backed away. He couldn't help them, just like he couldn't help Ian. He turned away and checked his watch. "I've got to hurry." Quickening his pace. "Besides, we need to go home to Kelly. She needs me and I can help her."

Boon trotted alongside him, holding up his front paw now showing signs he'd been gnawing at the bandage. Jace stopped and frowned at him, "And quit chewing on that." He scrutinized his paw and released it. The dog's tongue hung out, panting. He licked Jace's hand and tucked his head under it for a reassuring pat. Jace offered a strained smile and rubbed his hand down the dog. "Let's go."

Small quakes continued to shake the area, debris falling from buildings as they dodged broken windows and fallen signs. Trying to hurry, he continued his hop-walking down the middle of the street. Uneasiness clouded his senses, knowing the gang could be right behind them, but the sidewalks were littered, and bricks fell sporadically from buildings. The pace was slow, and so far, they'd barely covered a mile and half of the four miles to the house.

Jace, continuously eyeing his watch and checking his phone, watched the sky as it grew darker and walked along, neurotically thumbing the flap to his satchel.

A shrill scream pierced the air and Jace stopped, staring into the dark windows of the buildings around him. He grabbed Boon's leash and hurried to the side of a building peering out into the street. He did not want to tangle with that gang.

Again, the scream, like nails on a chalkboard, made him cringe, the hairs on his arms stood on end and he gritted his teeth against the shrill sound. A woman's scream, that was clear, but he couldn't place where the sound was coming from. He stood silent.

"Help me please...Somebody!"

His head jerked around to look behind, trying to identify what he heard. He spotted an area where the voice came from. It was coming from a side street. Indecision immobilized him and longingly he stared toward home.

The sobbing voice cried out again, only weaker this time. "Is anybody out there?" The now desperate voice choked and sobbed. "Please help me."

"Ugh." His gasp accentuated. "What now?" He turned and stomped off toward home, wincing at the pain from his ankle. He wasn't going to get involved. He didn't have time for this. Again, the voice cried out, this time a pathetic sob. Grabbing at his hair he stood silent, thinking. "Dammit." He turned, moving in the direction of the cry for help.

She wasn't far, stuck beneath a light pole, her bike pinning her to the pavement. A smashed car had plowed into the pole, bringing it down. A destroyed fire hydrant spewed water over her in rolling waves. Jace dropped his crutch and limped to the scene getting blasted with the hydrant water. "What happened?" he called over to her while checking the car's occupant. "He's dead." Jace's glance shifted to the now rising water and he surveyed the area for a way to release her. Pooling on the street, it would not be long before it flooded. She was already partially submerged in the deluge.

The hydrant was wedged beneath the front of the car, the pole across its hood extending outward, the light at the end tangled in the spokes of the wheel on her bike. She was wedged beneath the bike, pinned by the pole that held it firmly to the ground. He hobbled to the end of the pole. Grunting, trying to lift the thing off her, it was no use, the full weight of the pole rested on the frame.

"Please... Ack, help me." Gurgling and struggling to keep her head above the rising water.

He looked at the placement of the bike and the pole. He only needed to free her foot from the pedal, and she could wriggle out. He hurried to the driver's door and yanked it open. The man slumped over and Jace hopped backward grabbing at his chest as though the body had attacked him. He stood trying to steady himself and regain his composure, then reached in pulling the trunk lever.

Jace rummaged around the trunk of the car pulling up the carpet to reveal the spare tire. Beneath lay the car's jack. Not a great option but the small scissor jack would have to do. He placed the jack under the seat section of the bike frame and began to turn the crank.

She screamed, "The spokes are cutting into my ankle." Her face contorted, she grabbed for her leg.

Jace released the pressure, which only made things worse. Shifting to the other side he jimmied it under the crank to the pedal and began to raise the end, this time it released her foot. He dropped the handle and hopped to where she was and struggled to drag her from under the wreckage. Both dropped down on the grass in front of a nearby house.

Inside, a man peered at them through the window. When Jace made eye contact with him, he quickly closed the curtain. "Thanks for the help, buddy." He snorted and offered her a hand up. "Are you ok?"

"I think so." She rubbed her ankle, rolling it around to check how it felt. "I don't think it's broken." She stood on it and pursed her lips. "I'm ok... thanks to you." A crooked smile emerged, lighting up her face.

A bright red streak rolled down her forehead. She swiped at it and wrung her shoulder length fiery red hair. Jace's head tilted. "Are you bleeding?"

"Huh?" She checked herself for injury and found none, then chortled knowingly. "The red is a dye." She smirked embarrassed.

"Well, if you're ok, I need to go." He turned to leave, pulling his water bottle from his pack and holding it in the stream of water.

"Wait," she exclaimed, stepping over to him. "Where are you going?"

"Home, to my girlfriend." Panic strangled his voice. He screwed the cap on the bottle and returned it to his pack.

"Please don't leave me here." The desperation in her

voice rising an octave. "There is a gang here, they stole my purse and left me there. I can't stay here alone." She pleaded with him following behind as he walked over to where Boon found a good place for a drink and was lapping at the water.

"I can't help you anymore. I have to get to her, she's diabetic and pregnant. I can't..." His voice hitched and he looked away.

"I can just come with you, at least until we find some help. Please? I can help you...Just don't leave me here." Her wide eyes, filled with tears and looking to the sky, "It's going to be dark soon."

Jace's shoulders slumped. "I suppose." He turned back and scowled at her. "If you can keep up." She'd probably run laps around his gimpy walk but he needed to assert himself.

"I can," she promised. "I won't slow you down. My name's Rayne… Rayne James." She jabbed her hand at him.

He did not stop what he was doing or turn to her. "Jace Walker," he simply grunted at her with an awkward nod. Shoving the crutch under his arm, he grimaced when he put pressure on his ankle. He didn't want someone else to worry about, recalling his mother's words, "People are not worth it."

He hated feeling this way, hated her for making him feel this way. Anger chiseled his face, and he clenched his teeth as he hobbled down the street with Boon at his side and Rayne following close behind.

The sun waned in the distance, a dull orange glow against the clouds was all that remained of the day as the evening closed in and the impending darkness crept over the disintegrating city. His heart sank, knowing that everything would become that much harder in the dark. Trying to move through the city in the darkness would mask many dangers but he had to find Kelly.

He shuddered, a shiver racking his body. The night air was growing colder. He glanced at Rayne, who trailed along behind, never missing a step. She too was shivering. They were both wet and cold; her teeth chattering, she never complained once. His ankle screamed in protest with every step and even Boon looked weary.

"Listen, let's stop for a few to make a fire to warm up." He actually looked at her and her slumped shoulders showed that she was relieved. "The break will do us good, but only a short one to dry off. Ok?"

Rayne reached down and gathered up some loose papers and pointed to a parking garage across the road. Plenty of wood littered the streets amongst the debris and in no time, they'd gathered up an arm load. A warm fire was just what they needed. Nestled into a slot between two cars left on the second level made a great little cove. The cars blocked any breeze and allowed them to contain the heat and light from the fire.

Jace sat brooding holding a small box he'd retrieved from his satchel, turning it over in his hands. Speaking to Rayne and Boon but not looking up he mumbled, "Maybe another half hour and then it's time to get moving." He closed the box and put it back in the pack, retrieving the last of the jerky and crackers, and the water bottle. "Dinner, anyone?"

Rayne smiled warmly, accepting a slice of jerky and a couple crackers. Munching on a cracker and ripping off a chunk of the chewy meat between her teeth, she offered a thumbs up in approval.

SMASH

Below them laughter echoed as windows shattered in the night. Jace hurried to cover the fire light, smothering the flames with a small cloth painter tarp they'd found. "Let's go," he whispered.

They hurried as fast as Jace could move, propelling himself down the up ramp with his one crutch, and slid out on the far side. Taking streets left, then right, he became turned around with no idea how to find home in the dark. He couldn't place anything, the city dark with small arcs of electricity coming from transformers overhead. The sounds of the looters growing louder, he backed against the building and gripped his knees trying to catch a moment to think.

His eyes darting from side to side, anxiety was nearly overwhelming. The words, but a mere whisper, escaped his quivering lips. "Kelly, I'm trying babe. Where are you?"

Six

Cami

"I can't believe how hard it is to see." Cami flipped the wiper switch to high, squinting and looking up at the falling ash.

"Cami, look out!" Theo reached over and grabbed the wheel, pulling it hard. The Jeep swerved and thumped over the sidewalk slamming into a bike rack.

"What the hell Theo?" She shot him an accusatory look and scowled at him. "My dad's gonna kill us."

"There." He pointed out the window. "There is an old man in the road," he gasped motioning to the man struggling to walk. "I think he needs help."

Cami's eyes widened and she covered her mouth with her hand. They hopped from the vehicle and ran to the man bent over coughing violently. Grasping his arms, they helped him to the side of the road.

"What happened to you?"

"I don't know," the man choked. "I just can't breathe."

Theo handed him a bandana to put over his mouth. "It's the ash, keep your mouth covered."

Cami wadded up her small accessory scarf and held it to her face, while Theo used his jacket. Once the man was safely across the street, Theo shoved the Jeep while Cami gunned reverse. A loud squeal pierced the air when the Jeep jerked backward, dislodging the vehicle from the rack and leaving it in a twisted heap.

On their way again, Cami's expression became less playful. "Do you think everything is going to be ok?"

"Oh this?" Theo scoffed. "I bet it will all pass by morning, and it will all be nothing but a bit of a mess to clean up." He smiled at her, but it was not sincere…He couldn't hide his fears, he too looked unsure.

They weaved through the streets, dodging crashes and shifting directions, until they came into an area where the quake had collapsed two buildings, shutting off any route through. Cami knew the streets, but she had ash in her eyes. They burned and everything was a big blur. "I can't see." Her fist was in her eye rubbing at it furiously.

"Stop! Stop right here." Theo reached into his bag and handed her some water. "Hop out, I'll drive. You can just tell me where to go."

She snickered, trying to hold in the giggle.

"What's so funny?"

"Oh, I'll tell you where to go alright." Her eyes were bloodshot and continued to tear up.

"Rinse your eyes with the water I gave you. Squirt 'em good to get the ash out of them."

He climbed into the driver's seat and glanced at her, dabbing her eyes with a tissue from the glove compartment. "Ok, where to?"

"Let me get my bearings." She blinked and squinted out the window trying to catch a glimpse of some landmark or sign. The whole area was riddled with issues. People coughing in the streets, buildings crumbling, car accidents, and injuries. Every time she thought they were on their way another issue would crop up and hamper their travel. "Go right, here."

Theo jerked the wheel and Cami fell into his lap. He smiled while she tried to right herself. She insisted on taking over the wheel again. A few false starts and wrong turns later and it wasn't long before they were rounding the corner to his complex. Cami slammed on the brakes throwing Theo into the dash.

"What the hell, Cami?" he said laughingly after she'd said it to him earlier.

She stared straight ahead without saying a word.

"What are you…" His eyes followed her gaze and the rest of the words caught in his throat. The building he'd just moved into was ablaze. Flames shot into the gray skies, and black smoke billowed upward, mixing with the clouds and ash.

"Was that your building?"

Theo nodded affirming her fears, but without expression. His face, like stone, just stared blankly at the blaze. "I don't know what to do." He turned to her, his eyes shifting right and left. "Maybe I can find a sofa back at the office?"

"Nonsense." Her fingers turned white, she gripped the wheel so tight. She knew he was far more lost than ever but wouldn't show it. She spun the Jeep around and returned the way they'd come.

"I don't have any place else to go," he objected, his voice near panic.

"You'll stay with us until this settles down. Besides, I don't even know if we could get back to DTC with the roads so bad. You're simply going to have to bunk in the spare room."

His gaze dropped to his hands folded in his lap. "I appreciate the hospitality," he murmured.

She released the steering wheel with her right hand and touched his. His face rose to meet her gaze. "If it had not been for you, I might be lying in the rubble with Blythe. I owe you. Besides, how would I have gotten home?" Her eyes turned mischievous. "How else am I supposed to earn the boss's favor at work?"

His brow furrowed slightly, and he tipped his head.

She winked at him and turned back to the road as though the day were perfectly normal. Expertly navigating the streets back to her father and brother, it wasn't long before they were parked in the garage. Theo's hand brushed the gray soot covering the vehicle as he rounded the bumper and rubbed it between his fingers.

"Curious."

"What is?" Cami stopped with her hand on the doorknob.

He held out his hand with the soot on it for her to see. "It feels strangely soft, but gritty."

Softly swiping some of the fine dust from his fingers she swirled it between her index finger and thumb, then sniffed it. Her eyebrows furrowed, drawing back the fine dust from her face. "It is kind of weird. Let's go in and see what dad thinks." She turned the knob and opened the door, stepping inside and waving at him to follow her. He reached back and wiped a bit more into his hand and followed her into the house.

Her father looked at her wide-eyed as they walked into the kitchen covered in the gray dust. "I thought you were taking him home. What happened?" He checked her up and down for injuries before standing in front of them both for information.

"Sir." Theo stepped forward, placing his arm around Cami's shoulder.

Her father looked suspiciously at him saying, "Don't

call me 'Sir'. What happened?"

Theo explained the man in the street, crashing the front of the Jeep and the damage across the area. Her dad was eyeing him as he moved forward recounting what they saw at his apartment. "I thought I might go back to the office, but Cami insisted I come here since that building was damaged in the quake. I hope it is not an imposition."

His stance relaxed and his head bobbed up and down slightly as he thought. "She's right and we do have the spare room. We might need the help before this is all over." Heading for the garage he motioned for him to follow. "We best have a look at the Jeep to make sure there is no serious damage."

Cami made for the spare room, her brother in tow asking question after question. "What was it like out there? Did you see anything? Did you know this is a volcano? Why are you covered in gray dust?"

"The dust," Cami exclaimed. "That's right." She made for the door to the garage, peering over her shoulder, she called out, "Joey can you grab the bedding for the spare room? I'll be right back."

Leaving him to fetch the items she hurried to the garage. "Dad, Theo… The dust!"

They looked up at her and then to one another. Finally the realization hit. If this was ash from the volcano, and if it was part of a super eruption, they may be too close to it.

Her father headed for the kitchen. "We need to find out exactly what is going on."

SEVEN

JACE

Jace cautiously leaned his head through the doorway from the back room into the ravaged storefront and then back to Rayne. "I still think we should have made a run for it."

"Not with that ankle, you weren't." She gave Boon a quick pat on the head and stood defiant with her arms crossed. "You should be taking advantage of this time and elevating it instead of dancing in front of the doorway."

"I'm keeping watch," he snorted. "We need to get moving as soon as the coast is clear." His foot banged into the doorframe when he turned, he winced and slowly put pressure on the sore ankle. She was right and he knew it. His ankle was getting worse, not better, and even with the tape the throbbing grew more intense.

Rayne pulled a chair over next to a small table and wadded up some rags to cushion his ankle and insisted he elevate it. "I will watch for a while." She shoved him aside and pointed to the chair. "Put that foot up or we aren't going anywhere."

"We? There is no we! I am going home to Kelly. I'm just wasting time here." His eyes narrowed and nostrils flared. "You can wait here and pray for better timing. I'm outta here."

"Come on now. Just relax." Rayne followed him to the front of the store, shoved past him, and leaned through the opening checking in both directions while he jammed the crutch under his arm and hobbled to the door. "Are you really going to do this?"

His burning gaze drilled into her, and he glared at her. It enraged him just standing there. He didn't even know why he was so mad at her; he was just mad. He wanted to get home to Kelly but the world around him seemed hell bent on keeping him from her. Every moment, praying that the baby was alright while his heart ached in fear that she wasn't home and he would have failed his son, just like his own father.

A shrill scream halted his steps. They both scooted back inside and dipped behind the store's checkout counter. Rayne pulled Boon close, squeezing him and knocking the air out of him making him grunt. She hugged him, burying her face into his fur while Jace dared to check around the counter. Four people stood outside the store. One girl rummaged through the articles of clothing strewn on the floor squealing at the high-end merchandise she'd found.

Jace turned back to Rayne putting his finger to his pursed lips whispering, "They're inside." He pointed to the backroom door and nodded for her to crawl over to it. She shimmied along the floor tugging on Boon's leash, but he stood fast and wouldn't leave Jace's side.

Boon's fur on his back stood on end and he growled. It was a low growl, barely audible. Jace tried to hush him by rubbing his muzzle. Boon bared his teeth and growled louder. "Shh boy," he cooed. Boon moved toward Jace still growling with a menacing look in his eyes. At that moment Jace worried that it was him the dog was growling at. His eyes wide he put his hands up to the dog. "Boon! What's wrong boy?"

The dog's eyes darted past Jace. A momentary glint caught his attention just before Boon lunged, barking, and snarling past Jace to the side of the counter. His massive jaws and sharp teeth latched on to the man's hand.

A long butcher knife clinked to the tiles, dropping as though in slow motion. The man fell backward with the large Rottweiler on top of him snarling. Boon bit at his jacketed arm flung up in protection, shaking and twisting it with terrifying strength. Another man rushed the dog, knife raised. A high heeled shoe shot across the room and hit the second man on the back of his head. Rayne threw another one, hitting the target. Jace grabbed the leash and jerked Boon away from the knife wielding men and back to him. Boon would not be restrained and attacked the man who lunged at them.

The two women stood at the entrance of the door yelling. The one with a pile of clothes over her arm shouted obscenities while the other just begged to go.

Jace stood, hopping, hands out in defense, with his crutch on the floor in front of him. "What's your problem man?"

The man swiped at the air with his knife. "You are." He pointed to his buddy still curled up cradling his arm. "I'm gonna kill that mutt for tearing up Eli over there."

The woman grasping the clothes to her chest danced excitedly near the window goading him. "Knife 'em, Johnny."

The other woman, who'd pleaded with them to go, hurried to the man on the floor and helped him up. The two headed for the door. Jace's shoulders relaxed briefly, but prematurely. Johnny was still taunting Boon, jerking his body in fake lunges, and laughing. Jace held him back by his collar, but Boon was writhing to escape it.

The man continued circling the knife dancing from hand to hand, he pointed it at Jace. "What's in the purse?"

Jace's face began to heat up and his hands shook; he'd had enough of this. "Go," he commanded. "Leave us alone. We haven't done anything to you." Johnny didn't move. Jace loosened his grip on Boon's collar with one hand but held it tighter with the other. Boon growled. "Go, or I'll set the dog on you too."

"Come on Johnny. Get 'em." The cackling woman

taunted with her words. "Just knife 'em and take the bag. Let's see what this beach bum has inside."

"Shut up!" He spun around, giving her the bird. "I'll take care of them when I want."

Jace reached for his crutch. Johnny's head turned back to Jace. His eyes bloodshot with his eyebrows merged together. They bored into Jace. His heart jumped in his chest and just as the man spun back around he raised the crutch knocking the knife wide. Immediately he released his grip on Boon. Boon leaped at the man latching on to his forearm and shaking his head violently, tearing away the light shirtsleeve and drawing blood. But Johnny was not a small man. He rolled over onto Boon and wound back with his fist ready to strike the dog.

Jace jumped on him wielding a stiletto shoe like a weapon. He plunged the heel deep into the man's shoulder knocking him off Boon. Jace and Boon grappled with the man on the floor who now only tried to crawl away from them.

Jace sat back on his heels, catching sight of Rayne slowly approaching the woman at the window with a high heel of her own poised to attack. The woman dropped her armload of clothes and turned, running out of the building. Johnny followed her, cursing behind at them, threatening to return.

Jace picked up his crutch and hobbled over to the counter area. "We better go. Let's get whatever we can and get moving." He retrieved the man's knife, shoving it into his satchel. "We may need this."

Rayne was ready to go now, too. It was a women's clothing store and she'd already found some leggings, a sports bra, a matching jacket, and a pair of running shoes. "Let me change real quick. I'll be right back." Without waiting for a response, she disappeared into the back room.

Jace's eyes rolled upward as though the ceiling of the store had answers to some unasked question. "We don't have time for this," he called out after her. "Hurry up, they might come back."

Moments later she reappeared and Jace spat a mouthful of water onto the floor in surprise. "You're the fastest changer in the west. Damn that was quick," he chortled slightly.

She curtsied as though she were on stage and grabbed a backpack purse off the rack. "Just in case we find stuff I need to carry." She pulled the paper out of it and put the few things from her pockets inside. "Ready?"

"After you." Jace bowed in response to hers and pointed to the back room. "Let's use the door to the alley."

They cautiously scanned the area before exiting and walked in the dark, skulking around corners and keeping to the shadows. Rayne tapped his shoulder. "Where are we going?" she questioned, pausing in front of the looted remains of a convenience store.

"My house… I need to get to Kelly. I told you all of this already." Jace limped forward.

"I know this, but do you even know where it is?" Rayne paused and held Boon with her. "Can you hold on a minute?"

Jace stopped and without even looking at her he yelled out. "You know? You're a real pain in the ass." He turned to her and his eyes bored into her, his patience nearing its end. "Why don't you just go on your way. Boon and I will be just fine."

Rayne grabbed a map from the rack in the broken window and threw it at him. "We're lost and you, like a typical man, can't even stop for directions."

"We are not lost!" Jace puffed out his chest and squinted at her, challenging her accusation. He *wasn't* sure but wasn't about to let her know that.

Rayne placed her hands on her hips and jutted out her chin. "Really?" Her smirk visible, even in the dark. "This is the second time we've passed this store. I remembered the maps in the window from the first time we passed." She stood defiant, hands on her hips.

He didn't know where he was. He'd never been in this part of town; he'd only been in the area a little over a year and often found himself lost. Even with a GPS, he could barely find his way around. Nothing was familiar, many of the buildings were crumpled, and there was no sun or anything to help them figure out which direction they were moving. The GPS on his phone wouldn't connect without a signal. His head hung as though all his hopes had just died. "You're right." His head drooped and his eyes moved to the map laying on the ground at his feet. "But this won't help us. It's a state map, it only shows the highways."

"Let's go inside and see if there are more maps. Maybe we can find one with the city streets." She stepped closer, picking up the one that lay at his feet. "No matter what, we need to rest, even if only for a little bit. You can't help her if you fall over from exhaustion."

The lump in his throat ached and choked his words as they came out. "But…You don't understand."

"I'm sure she is just as worried about you. Let's just stop for a bit and get our bearings. I can help." She climbed through the broken glass on the door. "Let me. You saved me, let me help you somehow."

He followed her, his heart heavy in his chest, and his head pounding. He was no closer to finding Kelly, he was tired, and his ankle screamed with every step. They climbed through the doorway and behind the counter sat a small desk chair. He flopped into it, hunching over with his head in his hands, the overwhelming feeling of hopelessness gripped him. "I just can't do this." Tears fell to the floor, and he openly cried.

Rayne and Boon stood watching while he fell apart. He didn't know what to do, maybe his mother was right. 'You won't make it.' He heard his mother's words as though she stood right next to him. He couldn't help the others. He wouldn't be able to help Kelly either. He mumbled under his breath between sobs, "Kelly, I'm so sorry I can't help you." Again, thumbing the flap to his satchel, he raised his head and wiped the snot that ran down his lip. "I can't help you, either."

"Then let me help you." Rayne's voice was softer and full of concern. "You're exhausted. Sit, put your foot up and rest. Boon and I will keep watch and look for a map that will show us the way."

Rayne placed a folded smock on the shelf under the counter for his foot to rest on and he laid his head back against the chair. His eyes closed and he listened, his hand unconsciously caressing the soft fur of the dog who'd placed his head in his lap. Soft rustling noises and the low hum of Rayne as she rummaged through what was left of the small store. His eyes were heavy, and tears ran down into his ears as the darkness closed in.

It seemed like only moments had passed before Rayne was whispering in his ear. "Jace... Jace, wake up." He heard her but was groggy, almost as though it were a dream. "Jace." She shook him.

"Wha?" He jumped. She held him down. He felt confused and disoriented, the place looked different. There was light.

"Shh, there are people outside the store. They've already been inside. They checked the register, but it was open on the floor, so they left." The voices became more distant as the group moved on. She handed him a bottle of water. "There are also bottles of cold coffee and tea. I needed some caffeine and snagged these. I brought over both, not sure if you liked either."

Jace grabbed the can of tea and cracked it open and took a long drink. "How long have I been asleep?"

"Hours." She crept toward the door. "At one point you began to snore, but Boon took care of that and licked your face."

He reached out for Boon; grateful he'd found him and squeezed his neck. "I'm glad we're friends." He stroked his head and scratched under his ears.

Rayne returned to where he was sitting with a pair of sweatpants and some hiker boots and socks. "Change, I think the boots will help stabilize your ankle and it looks like rain. Those sandals won't help. Let's get this wrap off and have a look at it."

Jace recoiled, pulling his foot off the shelf and slamming it to the floor. The pain in his ankle stunned him and he sat straighter gripping the arms of the chair.

Rayne unwrapped the haggard looking bandage. "Oh, give it to me, you big baby."

Jace was uncomfortable with her touching it. Soothing himself, his hand slowly ran down the length of Boon's back. Boon licked it and Jace felt his paw. It too had a fresh bandage. Green athletic tape wrapped neatly around it. He panicked and reached for his bag. It was hanging from his side. "Where'd you get this stuff?" None of it could have come from this small convenience store.

"I found a flashlight last night and a street map. I needed to find out what street we were on and went outside to the corner. Apparently, the whole area seems to be nothing but stores. There is a pharmacy up the street, so I popped in and grabbed some stuff for your foot." She opened the book of maps and pointed to a location on the map. "We are on West Dayton Street. Where do you live?"

Jace didn't know how long he'd been out, but the sun was beginning to rise. He grabbed the map from her and looked over the pages while she finished unwrapping his foot. "Eww." He looked over the top of the map to see her scrunching her nose. "What did you step in?" She cast off the nasty tape and began to shove a sock over his still dirty foot.

"Blood." He sat waiting for her reaction with tight lips. Her eyes widened momentarily, and he smugly returned to studying the map.

She wrapped the sports tape over the sock and placed his foot on the floor. He stood testing out the ankle. It felt less sore and stronger. She reached for his shorts. "Ok, time to change out of these so you can get the boots on." He grappled with the waistband pulling them upward. She tipped her head to him, stood, and moved to the rack at the end of the counter. "Fine then, I wasn't gonna look. Get changed and let's figure out how to get you home." Grabbing a handful of nuts and shoving them into her purse pack she turned her back on him to let him change.

He'd been mean to her and here she helped him. Jace was embarrassed and humbled all at once. "Listen Rayne, I'm uh... Well..."

She paused to look at him, standing there, his arms hung limply at his sides. "Yeah, yeah, I get it. But you remember this," she warned him, yet smiled slightly. It was a weak and troubled smile; one he was unsure if it was actually a smile or a grimace.

She turned back to the racks, collecting items from the store and grunted, waving him off to change. He pulled up the sweatpants. "I'm sorry for the things I said last night."

"I know." She faced him, a tear in the corner of her eye. "I'm not from here. I'm a student at City College. My dad lives in Denver, but I haven't been there in a couple years. I have no one here and I'm scared." Tears ran down her cheeks. "Please don't leave me out here alone. I heard the people talking and the area was evacuated yesterday because of tsunamis as well as some kind of giant pile up on the 210."

"That explains it." Jace's face lit up. "Pasadena is mostly protected from this due to the mountains. Ventura was all backed up from a bridge collapse near Arroyo. I had to go around it and that is where I found you." He slapped the map open on the counter. "We live in Lacy Park on South Oak Knoll." He pulled the boots on and marveled at the perfect fit. "How'd you know my size?"

She offered a small smile and kicked over his sandal, the size marked in a small circle on the bottom. He stuffed his satchel with a few extra water bottles, some beef jerky sticks, and grabbed a Ho-Ho. He was ready to go. His ankle felt stronger and the weight on it wasn't so bad. He picked up the crutch and walked to the opening with Rayne and Boon right behind him.

Rayne reached up to his shoulder lightly touching it. "Let's go get Kelly."

His head tilted in quick acknowledgement, and they headed up the street toward where Rayne directed him. Pointing out Fair Oaks Street. Jace had needed some rest, he was renewed and determined to get to Kelly. She was surely home by now. He envisioned her sitting on the sofa at home and the corners of his mouth turned upward momentarily. "You know. I bet she is home right now." With the new boots and stronger ankle, his step quickened.

The street was deserted, but they walked cautiously down Fair Oaks. At Central Park he waved his arm at Rayne. "Let's cut through the park." Boon ran into the grassy area and turned to face them, his hind end up and front paws stretched out low in front. Playful and leaping side to side. Suddenly the world did not feel so terrible and Jace would soon be home with Kelly and the baby.

None of them were paying attention until a deep voice rang out. "You there. Where are you going?"

Jace stopped dead in his tracks, dread rolling down his spine, frozen. His anxiety rose and gripped him and he squeezed the handle of the crutch. Ready for anything. He slowly turned in the direction of the voice. Two police officers approached them. Rayne hurried over to him dragging Boon by his leash. Boon growled and the man pointed his gun at the dog. Jace hurried to one knee in front of Boon. "He's not mean, just protective." His hand up toward the man he hugged Boon around his neck with the other. "I've got him."

"I asked you a question." The man eyed them up and down, spending a little too long on Rayne.

"I'm going home to my girlfriend. She's just over in Lacy Park. It's only about a mile or so." Jace paused expectantly and when there was no response he continued, "Maybe you could give us a ride? She might need help. She's pregnant and a diabetic."

The men continued to eye them without a word until the second one spoke. "That whole area has been burned out. Why don't you come with us?"

"No," Jace cried out. "I've got to find her."

EIGHT

THEO

Darkness fell across the city. The ash from Dotsero had subsided and Theo sat uncomfortably across from Cami. They all gathered around the table with him, Cami, and her family together. Each had thoughts on things but what they needed was to consider what to do. He wasn't in charge there and his discomfort showed to everyone. He gwaffed at Joey's suggestion that aliens were using a powerful beam to spawn the earthquakes and volcanoes. By the way he fidgeted in his seat, Cami noted his discomfort and frowned. The silence was killing him and finally he spoke. "So, I think the worst might be over."

"Maybe." Cami's dad interjected immediately, his head bobbing up and down and eyebrows coming together. He placed his palms on the table; rose and turned to the kitchen. His less than agreeable demeanor showed when he glanced side eyed at Theo and Cami; no one would ever be good enough for his little girl.

All was fine when she was bringing him home but now that he must stay, Doug was only slightly irritable, but enough that both Theo and Cami noticed it. The icy edge in his voice made Theo uneasy.

Cami reached for his hand across the table, and he jerked it back like she'd stung him. It shocked her and her eyebrows raised in question. "I just wanted to get your attention."

"I'm sorry." He looked down. "It's just…"

"I know…it's Dad. He's always like this, don't worry about it. If he really didn't like you, you would know it."

"It feels pretty obvious."

Joey snorted, and Cami glared at him. "Don't you start."

"What? I didn't say anything." He held his hands up at her.

"You didn't have to, now knock it off. Everything is bad enough without your attitude."

Doug returned to the table with a small radio and began twisting the knob to tune it into a station. A few moments of static, some beeping, and the emergency alert signal was all he could find. He shoved it over and slumped back into his chair.

Cami hopped up and hurried to the end of the table kneeling next to him. "Dad, what's wrong? It's just a small radio, probably just can't pick up the stations, that's all."

"It's not that," he sighed. "It's just this feeling I've got in the pit of my stomach. Something is just nagging at me about all of this. The volcano has stopped but we are still getting tremors. I haven't heard from your sister at all." He looked away, "I knew letting her go to California was a mistake."

"Perhaps volcanoes have aftershocks like earthquakes do." Theo rose and peered out the window into the darkness, his dad was in California. The man rode him his whole life, he could never be good enough. Ever since his mom left, his dad made his life hell. But deep inside Theo knew it was more about her than him. He once told him that he wouldn't have him be a quitter like his mother. He smacked his leg with his fist in anger, staring out the window, emotions in a twist. Torn between wishing a volcano decimated his father's company and worrying for him.

The power was out, and their small lanterns didn't shed light on much of anything beyond the room they were in. An orange glow in the distance troubled them. It was hard to tell how far off and how big the fire was, but it was substantial. Without any help from emergency services, they worried it could burn through half the city before it stopped. In the arid Denver climate things tended to burn hot and fast.

"Can you see anything?" Cami asked, walking to stand beside Theo at the window.

"Nah Cami, the other houses and buildings block the view. If only we could get some elevation, we might catch a glimpse of the area." He shoved his hands in his pocket and turned away from the window.

"I have an idea." Joey hopped up from his seat and grabbed his shoes. "C'mon." He waved them to follow, bolting for the door to the back yard. He halted right outside and called back over his shoulder. "Come on! We can get a better view."

Both hurried for the door and followed him into the yard. The ladder to the small tree house was barely visible in the blackness but Joey led them right to it. In seconds he was at the top reaching for Cami's hand. She gripped the ladder and hesitantly began to climb. They scaled the ladder and stood peering out the small window into the night.

Cami's hands went to her mouth, and she struggled to constrain the gasp. Theo stood silently gazing across the landscape. Peering through one window and then to the next, trying to take in the full three-hundred-sixty-degree view of their situation.

Not two blocks away a large residential area was fully engulfed, and the wind was coming their way. "This is not good," Joey blurted out. "Not good at all. Cam we gotta go tell dad."

"Ok, yeah. You're right Joey. Let's go." The words seemed stuck in her throat as she turned to follow.

Joey scurried down the ladder in record time landing hard at the bottom, grunting and racing for the house. Just as Cami was about to begin her descent Theo's cell phone rang and startled them both. She paused looking up at him as his hands fumbled with the device trying to swipe the screen and answer it.

"Theo, here," he panted into the phone speaker. "What? I can't hear you. Can you say that again?"

He stood silent as the voice boomed loud enough for Cami to hear it. Struggling to keep the sound coming through, his eyes darted around the small tree house.

"But…"

The voice grew louder, and Cami couldn't help but overhear although she tried to pretend that she wasn't listening. Theo could see she'd heard, and his eyes fell to the floor. Searching as though there were some revelations tucked neatly between the boards that could save him.

"Theodore, I told you… Didn't I tell you? You never listen. Would you look at the mess you've made of your life?"

"But Dad, it's an excellent job and there's room to advance."

"Your place is in the company, here. Why do you think I paid for all that damn schooling? With all of this going on, I needed you here."

"I wanted…"

"You're such a disappointment to…"

The line went dead, and Theo seemed relieved. His hand with the phone dropped to his side and he sighed. Cami tried to be coy about the whole thing and pretend she didn't hear anything, but Theo was troubled, his father's tone was off. Theo had listened to his father's criticism all his life but this time it was more, almost begging him to come home. Something was bothering his father and something big enough to bother him was big!

Theo turned to Cami and motioned her down the ladder. She hopped down, skipping the last two rungs and waited for him to follow.

Theo slowly descended the ladder pausing on the last rung. He turned abruptly, noting her staring at him. The air rushed across his lips, and he approached her. "Something is very wrong."

"Well yeah!" she quipped. "Half the city is on fire. I'd say that was pretty wrong. Do you think it will reach us?"

"I don't mean that. I mean…yeah that is wrong. But the phone call… That was my dad."

"Oh?" Cami feigned surprise.

"I know you heard him."

"Yeah." She looked down at her feet.

"He is freaked… I mean really freaked. It was in his voice; the level was almost a panic."

"I guess anyone would be. Who would have thought there would be a volcano in Denver?"

"He's not in Denver."

Cami scrunched her eyebrows tilting her head. "Where is he?"

"La Jolla."

"Where's that?"

"California."

"Ok?" Cami turned to go into the house.

Theo reached for her arm and turned her back. "Don't you know what that means?"

"What?"

"That this event is bigger than just here. It's worse than we could have thought. It could be everywhere."

Cami's eyes widened. "Everywhere?"

"We need to find a way to get more info. C'mon." He snatched her hand and practically ran for the house.

NINE

JACE

"Jace," Rayne warned. "Jace, we need to be smart about this. If we take off running, you won't get fifty feet and they'll just follow us. Let's just go along and watch for a chance to sneak away."

"No! I can't," he pleaded. "What about Kelly?" His nostrils flared, anger seething. Turning away to avoid her eyes. He knew she was right but wouldn't accept it, he couldn't.

She drew closer and whispered behind him into his ear. "We have eyes on us." She placed her hands on his shoulders and felt him shudder. "You've got to get it together and pretend to give in and accept this. We won't give up." She drew closer, "I'm going to start talking louder, reasoning with you that she is likely there already."

"But..." He drew back.

"Will you just listen to me, dammit?"

He nodded and slouched his shoulders. He was defeated and tired, but he trusted her already. Rayne had been a huge help to him, and he knew she only wanted to help. It was even likely he would not have made it this far without her help. It was barely morning but he wanted nothing more than to reach Kelly.

In a louder tone she began, checking to make sure the men heard her. "I know you're worried, but I would almost guarantee that she is safe and sound wherever they are taking us. She is probably waiting for you there."

"You really think so?" He turned and tried to look hopeful.

"Look around us. They cleared the area, and this means they would have found her and brought her there, too."

Jace glanced around as though he were surveying the area, his head bobbing up and down slightly. "Perhaps you're right. There doesn't seem to be anyone around. Maybe we could ask?"

Rayne did note the man moving closer and wanted to make it good. "I would think they have a list of all the people they've rescued."

Something was off about these two guys and they both knew it. At first Jace could not understand why Rayne wanted to go along with them, but he quickly figured out that she, too, felt it. One glance at the man headed their way gave off an alarm not only with the two of them but Boon also. At first, they wanted them to just leave Boon to fend for himself but soon found that Jace would not have it. The second guy stepped in and said they were allowing pets, but that he had to stay on his leash.

Their manner was off, the way their clothes fit was off, the way they communicated and even their movements were off.

Rayne's glance turned to Jace, and she whispered, "Something isn't right. My uncle was in the National Guard and would never look so sloppy."

Jace agreed with her. He felt like this was something different and the only way out was to go along until the chance to get away presented itself.

"Excuse me, sir?" Rayne moved toward the man.

"Ma'am?"

"Would you have a list of all those that you've rescued?"

He stammered for a moment and the second man stepped in. "Yes, of course we do." His answer was snide and cool with an edge of annoyance.

Rayne excitedly turned to Jace and stepped up next to him, giving Boon a quick scratch behind his ear. "See? I told you they would know."

She looked back to the men and thanked them, moving off and away trying to gain some distance but they swiftly jumped in her direction. "Ma'am, where are you going?"

"Wha?" She looked back. "Oh," a slight giggle and she pointed to their small pile. "To grab our things over here."

"Oh, ok. Please be quick about it."

Jace turned to follow her thinking she planned to escape now but the man grabbed his arm. Boon growled and bared his teeth. Jace looked at them and calmed Boon. "I was just gonna help her."

"I got it." The second man moved quickly after her.

Jace had to strain to hear them, but Rayne played him like a violin. He watched as she sashayed over to the pack and leaned down suggestively as though it were a struggle. The man hurried to take it from her.

Jace just about coughed when she smiled at the man as he grabbed one of the packs. "Thank you," she cooed.

His look was quizzical, eyebrows raised, he tilted his head. "Is that your boyfriend?"

They weren't that far away and Jace leaned to hear as he stroked Boon's back.

"Jace?" She looked over her shoulder. "Oh, no he's not, but he did rescue me. You know I nearly drowned? He's hung up on some chick named Kelly, that's why he wanted to go."

"I see." The man's eyes narrowed, sending a shiver

down her spine.

"But… I'm sure you already rescued her." Rayne pointed toward a different section of the city on the far side of the park. "They lived over there."

"Oh sure, we already cleared that area."

Rayne smiled innocently at the man. Her plan to lay the misdirection for when they'd get out of there was good and Jace gave the slightest nod when she shot a glance at him.

The hope was to keep them searching in another area and it looked like it may have worked. A feeling gnawed at Jace still, he and Boon were the ones that weren't safe. She wasn't either but they wanted her alive and deep in his soul he knew why, and it made his blood boil. They would need to get out fast. And before these guys met up with any of their buddies.

She smiled sweetly at the man again, while the look in her eye was pure disgust.

The summer heat was nearly unbearable, and Rayne feigned heat fatigue asking where the camp was. Jace limped over to her just as she threw him a sly wink, and he poured on the injury, limping more noticeably.

"Lord, it's hot." She waved her hand in front of her face, fanning herself. "Do you think we could rest a while? Just until the sun sets, and it cools off a little bit. I'm afraid I might faint."

Jace watched her play them, getting them hopping

and tripping over one another to get her a piece of cardboard to use as a fan and bottle of water. If he wasn't so worried about Kelly, he may have busted out laughing.

Before long the two men were beginning to bicker. Jace overheard them, they'd been fighting over who would go first. His fists clenched as he led Boon to a nearby tree to settle in for a bit. He didn't like leaving Rayne over there with these two, but she'd insisted. Both he and Boon kept a keen eye on her, barely even blinking, as she skillfully played them one against the other. It wasn't long before there was a fist fight between the two, with Rayne pretending each was her choice. That she needed saving one from the other.

"Damn, she's good." Jace looked at Boon and petted his head. "But be ready buddy, one of them will win this and then it's about her. I hope she knew what she was doing."

He was right. It didn't take long before the one that was helping her with the bags was stabbed by the meaner one. He lay bleeding gasping for air calling out for her, but she scurried over to the man who'd won.

"What the hell is she doing?" Jace gripped Boon tighter, the low growl getting louder from the agitated dog.

"Oh, my, but you are strong," she purred at the man. "Can I feel?"

He held up his bent arm for her to admire, and before he knew what was happening, she plunged a long carving knife between his ribs and deep into the side of his chest.

Her knee came up full force slamming into his nuts with all she had before she snatched their bags from where she'd been sitting and screamed as she ran toward Jace. "RUN!"

Jace and Boon hopped up and took off to meet her. He grabbed his bag and slung it over his shoulder, running for all he was worth hopping with every other step. The pair darted down an alley in the area she'd said they were going. They climbed a dumpster and hopped over a fence before backtracking to go in the right direction. It was work to get Boon under the fence but at least it wasn't tall.

The boots Rayne had gotten him were really paying off with the support on the ankle and Jace was able to keep up. Rayne slowed and stood hunched over with her hands on her knees gasping for air. She choked in some air and coughed before vomiting on the pavement in front of her. "Sorry." She stood wiping her mouth. "Did you know what they were planning?"

"I had an idea." Jace's eyes narrowed, and he gritted his teeth. "Boon and I were both on edge."

Rayne knelt and reached out for Boon and wrapped her arms around his big furry neck, nuzzling into him. "What a good boy." Kneeling there petting the dog, her breathing slowed. "Are you ready to go get Kelly?"

Jace smiled slightly, reaching out for her hand to help her up. "Thanks to you. If you're ready, let's go."

Rayne stood and brushed the dirt from her knee and looked expectantly at him. "Which way?"

"Well, it's another six or eight blocks that way." His finger raised in the air pointing down the main road.

"We can't just go strolling up Broadway. We better look at some alleyways to travel."

"Broadway? That's not Broadway. It's…"

Rayne laughed, "I know it's not. It is just an expression."

Jace's face flushed. He was embarrassed that he didn't get her joke and he looked away from her.

"It's ok city boy, let's go get your girl. Shall we?"

TEN

CAMI

Cami's look was troubled, her forehead wrinkled with worry. Not for the fires in the city but for her sister. Theo's father was in California and he was worried, and Cami had no way to contact Rayne. She glanced at her father as Theo was recounting what his father had said in the phone call.

"Do you think we could call out?" Doug leaped from his chair and hurried toward the window.

"I'm not sure," Theo said hesitantly. "It's worth a try, but someone has to have service on the other end."

"Hey how come you have service on your phone but none of us do?" Joey narrowed his eyes at Theo.

"Oh, right. This is a satellite phone. My father's company uses them, and he insisted I have one before coming to Denver."

"What is a satellite phone?" Joey closed in on it, peering as though it might bite him.

"Instead of getting signal from the cell towers there is a satellite in space that relays the signal."

"Oh, now that's cool," he grinned. Snapping his head toward his father he was nearly giddy. "Kinda like some Trekkie gadgets, huh dad?"

"Yeah, I guess." Doug was pensive and worried about his daughter.

"Let's go and try to call her." Theo urged him toward the door.

"Cami can do it." He looked at her pleading. "Find her?"

"I'll try."

They returned to the treehouse to get a better signal; Theo assured them that it didn't make a difference. Cami nodded but she wanted to keep an eye on the fire anyway. Once back in the treehouse Cami pulled out her phone for the number and read it off to Theo who dialed. He passed her the phone saying, "Just hit send, same as any other phone."

Cami listened as Rayne's voicemail recounted the instructions. It finished off with, "Now, wait for the beep." A moment passed and it beeped, Cami sighed and hung up.

"Why'd you do that?" Theo reached for her hand with the phone hitting redial. "Leave a message at least so she knows this number can reach you." He listened as it rang and handed it to her. "Here."

Cami listened again and waited for the beep to sound. "Hey Rayne, it's Cam. If you get this message, we are all ok. Worried about you though. If you get service call us at..." She looked up at Theo for the number and recounted it in the message. "Rayne," she sniffed. "Come home... Please?"

She hung up and passed the phone back to Theo. Gazing out the window her voice monotone. "Looks like the fire changed direction."

"Yeah, that's what I was thinking. We may be ok... For now."

"Let's head back inside." She grasped the handle for the ladder and turned to descend.

They went back to the house and told Doug they'd only gotten voicemail but could try tomorrow. Theo tried to convince him that power outages could have cell service down and tomorrow might have better luck. Doug didn't believe him but patted him on the shoulder and passed by toward the family room with a nod.

No one could sleep although they each tried. Gunshots and explosions rocked the night and they watched out the windows in terror. Each of them took turns at the windows keeping watch over the fire, but also in the street. Although for what— No one really knew.

"Perhaps we should go for supplies in the morning." Doug looked at Theo nodding at him.

"That is probably a promising idea. I don't know how long things are going to be like this."

"Listen Theo, you are welcome to stay here with us until this all blows over." Doug reached his hand out to Theo.

"Thank you, Sir. I really appreciate that. I honestly have no idea where I would go."

"That is... as long as you don't call me 'Sir'."

They both shared a chuckle before Doug excused himself. Cami walked over to Theo, casting a sideways glance while her gaze followed her father into the kitchen.

"What was that all about?"

"Nothing, he just offered to let me say till it all blows over." Theo's look was troubled, and he turned to watch Doug pull some breakfast items together. He turned back to Cami. "I think he's really worried. I know he is upset about your sister, but this is something more."

"Yeah, I get that too." She paused and then looked up at him. "Way to make an impression on the new boss, huh? First, I poke fun with the Teddy Three comment then my city collapses around you. I hope this doesn't give you a bad taste for the company." She smirked at him.

"Well Miss James, I don't know but I believe we may have to discuss your future with the company." He smiled and reached for her hand, gently holding it. "In all seriousness, I am so grateful to you and your family…for everything."

She smiled awkwardly at him and nodded. "How about some breakfast?"

He dropped her hand and held his out for her to lead the way to the kitchen, following close behind her. Once they entered a woody salted smell reached them and Cami grinned in his direction, her eyebrows waggling.

"Bacon…"

"Oh man, that smells so good. This is awesome!" Theo excitedly pulled up to the table next to Joey, awaiting the food. A long sniff of the air and he exhaled loudly. "Oh, now that is truly an amazing smell. Am I smelling coffee, as well?" He looked at Cami and she smirked again, shaking her head at him.

"Don't ask…but yeah it's coffee."

Doug placed plates of bacon, scrambled eggs and hash browned potatoes on the table with a large pot of very strong coffee and a jug of orange juice.

"I figure we should eat up what is in the fridge, if the power doesn't come on soon it'll spoil."

Again, Theo sniffed and grinned. "This looks great! Thank you, Sir…. Ummm… Mr. James."

Doug chuckled, "It's just Doug, unless you want me calling you Teddy Three?"

Theo shot a look at Cami and Joey giggled. "I heard you in the living room," he snorted before reaching for the OJ.

Doug glanced from Theo to Cami and back to Theo. "I think this is a story I'd like to hear sometime."

Cami reached for the coffee and looked at her plate. "Nothing really, just a dumb comment."

Theo chortled. "It was the funniest thing I think has ever happened to me." He paused and looked at Cami. "She is intriguing, I will say that. I'll have to tell you about it later."

Cami grunted and glared at him with warning.

The sun was obscured by the ash in the clouds combined with the smoke from the fires. But an orange hue illuminated the horizon and finally morning had come. It was decided after breakfast that Theo and Cami would go for supplies, while Doug and Joey fortified the house. Doug hadn't said anything the day before, but he went to the safe in his small office and retrieved two handguns.

Joey caught sight of them in his dad's hands as he walked from the office and whistled loudly. "Well now, aren't those a couple beauties?"

"Don't even think about touching them."

"Geez, I wasn't gonna."

"I've kept these for many years." Doug glanced down at each in his hands, turning them over to admire them. "I'd planned that someday you and I might go to the range together."

"Really?" Joey stepped in to join his father in admiring the pair.

Cami looked up at him, puddles lingering on her lower lids. Fear and anguish tearing at her inside, yet she said nothing.

Theo reached for her and drew her close. She sobbed into his chest for a few moments, straightened, and quickly backed away. "I'm sorry," she sniffed. "It's just that... Rayne. All of this just feels so terrible. Will we ever see her again?"

"I'm sure you will. I have to believe that. My dad is out on the west coast too, remember? We will see them."

She smiled and nodded, grasping the keys from the hook and turning to go. Her father thrust one of the pistols at her. "Keep it in the car with you... Just in case."

"Dad...I don't..."

Theo reached for it, nodding to Doug. "I went to the range all the time with my dad. I'll take it." He pulled the slide back slightly to check for a round and then flipped it over glancing at the trigger. "A Glock, huh?"

"You know your guns. Good to know, I feel safer now having her scouting with you already." Shifting his gaze to his daughter. "Cam, you have the list?"

"Right here," she said, patting her back pocket.

"Don't be too long, ok?"

They both acknowledged him as they headed for the garage. Cami climbed into the Jeep while Theo opened the garage door. Cami started it and rolled out into at least an inch of light gray ash leaving tire tracks that looked as though they'd gotten fresh snow. Doug waved as he closed the door, mouthing 'Thank you' to Theo as they pulled away. Theo tipped the barrel of the gun in a salute and tucked it into his belt.

The streets were for the most part deserted. All but for the emergency vehicles that whizzed by, and the occasional car hurrying toward the highway, the city looked like a ghost town. Theo watched out the window as Cami drove toward the store. His eyes caught glimpses of figures in windows eyeing them as they drove by. The city was not deserted, in fact, more windows than not had figures peering out into the hazy and surreal scene.

"Do you think the stores will even be open?" He turned to Cami and motioned to the lifeless landscape.

"Honestly? I don't really know." She looked at him briefly. "I hadn't even considered that they would not be."

They turned into the huge lot to Kroger and found that the doors were open. There were no lights, but people were coming and going.

"Well… That's a good sign." Cami smiled at him. "Let's go." She opened the door and hopped down from the Jeep.

"Let's be quick about it." Theo warned, walking around the back of the Jeep and glancing at the people who were coming out of the store and then to a group of guys in the same parking lot near the Subway sub shop.

It didn't take them long to gather supplies. In the cart were things like water, dry and canned goods, duct tape, a box of heavy-duty trash bags. There was soda for Joey and a bottle of wine for Cami along with some beer and bourbon for her dad. They didn't go for much in the refrigerated section, unsure of how long the power would be out, but did make sure to grab as many of the snack bars they could find. Cliff bars were the most plentiful and these would last and be lightweight if they had to leave.

The man at the register had a small calculator and a price book with each item. The process was painstakingly slow, but Cami was careful to help by grouping items together and in sections. Pasta, the snack bars, and canned vegetables were all placed together in like kind. Corn, peas, green beans of the same brand would be the same price she surmised.

Theo held out his credit card to pay for the items and the young man looked at him furrowing his brow. "Sorry sir, cash only."

Theo felt awkward as he fished through his wallet for cash. He generally carried very little and was suddenly very aware of this mistake.

Cami reached for his arm and smiled. "Dad knew…" She pulled out an envelope with cash in it and paid for the supplies.

Once outside Theo started to object but Cami calmed him. "Listen, when this is all over, I'm sure you can shower us with whatever you feel you need to, but right now, I am happy with the strong arm to heft these bags." She grinned teasingly and gave his bicep a squeeze while eyeing him approvingly. She giggled at his confused look and motioned for him to get to work loading the supplies.

Cami's laugh made Theo's posture seem less uneasy about his now lack of money as well as a place to live and the two made jokes while loading the bags.

"Oh my, you are strong, sir." she exclaimed in a southern belle accent and feigned difficulty with the heavy bag.

"Knock it off, Cami," Theo laughed.

Cami turned quickly with the cart to return it to the store and abruptly stopped when she ran into someone. The man stood before her eyes narrowed, grasped the cart and shoved it back at her.

"Oh, excuse me," she apologized. "I didn't see you."

Theo came up beside her about the same time she recognized him. "Rob? Rob Stearns… is that you? Sorry, I didn't recognize you. Must be this gray light… Isn't this something?" She began to go on about the events and then realized he was glaring at Theo. "I'm sorry did you get to meet the…"

Rob cut her off. "I see you are working your way up in the company. What's the plan? You're gonna sleep your way to the top?"

"Wha…?" Cami gasped

"Hey now," Theo objected. "That is uncalled for."

"Maybe if you hadn't been busy flirting with the new boss man back at the office Blythe would still be alive."

Cami began to cry. "What are you talking about?"

"That's enough!" Theo stepped between them. "It was no one's fault…the balcony collapsed. Now back off."

"Oh look, the boss man protecting his little slut." He leered at her around him and never saw the right coming.

Theo plowed his fist into the man's jaw, knocking him to the ground. He stood over Rob, fist clenched as he scrambled for footing crab crawling backward. "I said…back off."

Rob backed away cursing. "Bitch," he shouted and glared at her.

Theo started after him, but Cami grabbed his arm. "What do you think you're doing?"

"I… Uh…"

"I don't need you to fight my battles." She angrily stomped over to the Jeep and whipped the door open. "Now everyone at work will think exactly what he said."

Tears rolled down her face as she stood in front of the door to the vehicle. "Let's go," she whimpered.

Theo was more confused than ever, but completely enamored with her now, she was a strong woman, yet still vulnerable. He stared out the window in silence as they made their way back to the house thinking about what the guy had done to her. There was something more to it, but he didn't dare ask her about it at the moment.

ELEVEN

JACE

Rayne's forearm was bleeding from the gash she'd gotten climbing over the fence, the jagged top left a nice long scratch from her elbow to her wrist and Jace used a long strip from his shirt to wrap around it.

"We're going to need to clean this and cover it properly."

She sucked air across her teeth as he tied the knot in the makeshift bandage. "Damn that stings."

"It's not deep, luckily, but it is pretty raw." He winced for her as he tucked the ends into the bandage.

"I should have shimmied under like Boon here." She winked at the panting dog and ruffled his ears. "Anyway, I think we lost them. Shall we go and find Kelly?"

Jace stood and reached out with his hand to help her up. She grabbed hold and lurched forward when he yanked falling into him. "Geeze Rayne, what do you weigh? Like six pounds?"

She laughed at him while brushing the dirt off her ass. "You just don't know your own strength." She paused and looked up at him. He'd gone quiet and was looking at the ground. "C'mon now, let's go get her, Ok?"

Rayne reached down and grabbed for her small pack and jumped when her phone began to ring. Shock and excitement rolled over her and she dropped it digging through the contents, eventually tipping it over and dumping them onto the ground. "Finally," she sighed. Swiping the screen to answer. The ringing stopped. She stared at the number and couldn't place it.

"Who was it?" Jace asked her.

"I don't know. Probably warning me about my car's extended warranty." She giggled a little and Jace burst out laughing. It was just what he needed to lighten things up.

"The world is crashing down, better make sure that warranty is good to go," he snorted and reached for his own pack. "Good one, Rayne. Let's get a move on."

She smiled and reached for her own pack but deep down wondered who'd called her. The phone was at two percent and the power was out. She chided herself for not charging it and shoved it into the pack.

Bwee Boop

The voicemail chimed, Jace stopped dead in his tracks while Rayne pulled the phone back out and opened her voicemail. She put it on speaker so they both could hear it. "Ray, Ray… It's Cam, if you get this message, we are all ok. Denver is pretty bad, but can you come home? We are worried about you. Call me back at…" The phone went dead.

"What happened?" Jace stepped closer.

"Phone died."

Jace reached for his own phone and pressed the unlock and tried to call Kelly while they had service. He listened expectantly, waiting. "Hi ya… I can't come to the phone, but you know what to do…" Beep…

"Kelly? Kelly, I'm coming." He hung up the phone and turned to Rayne. "Let's go."

Rayne followed but something about the voicemail bothered her. It was Cami's voice. Camilla was the calmest, most level headed person she knew, and this was not calm. Her call sounded panicked and uneasy. "Hey Jace?"

"Yeah," he said, without looking back to her, still trotting toward home.

"Something about her voicemail bothered me." She hurried up beside him. "Slow down will ya."

He paused and looked at her. "I want to get to Kelly. What's up?"

"She said, 'Denver is bad, but we're ok.'"

"Yeah? So?"

"Why would Denver, all the way on the other side of

the Rocky Mountains, not be ok?"

"Wha—?"

"Something is going on Jace." Panic rising in Rayne's voice. "I don't think all this...." She waved her arms around the destruction. "I mean, I don't think it is only here."

Somewhere in both of their minds they'd thought this was a local event. It never occurred to Jace that it was bigger. Panic gripped his chest and he bent over, leaning on his knees to catch his breath.

"Jace?"

"What?" His gaze shifted back to Rayne. "Right, let's go."

She reached for his arm, halting his march momentarily. "Listen, we'll find her. Ok?"

He glanced back at her and dipped his head before turning and heading toward home. His ankle was still in bad shape, but the boots Rayne found him were a lifesaver, at this point he was able to walk without the crutch which made navigating the debris much easier. Not a word passed between them as they climbed over smashed cars and skirted the occasional wandering person. Determination etched in Jace's brow and pushed him forward. Rayne followed, blankly observing the destruction. They were not far from Jace's home, but the hazards slowed them. It was already midday and they still had blocks to go.

Boon yelped, halting both of them. Jace spun around and lurched toward him to see what was wrong. He stood with his paw raised, a few drops of blood on the cement below.

"Dammit."

"What's wrong?" Rayne hurried over to help.

"His paw is bleeding again. He keeps ripping off the bandage."

Frustration clawed at Jace, he glanced in the direction of home, yet they had to wait and do something with his paw. Rayne quickly emptied supplies from her pack and sprayed the paw, blowing on it. Boon whimpered slightly but Jace scratched behind his ears.

"This is bad." Rayne glanced up at him.

"It was how we met." Jace continued to rub the dog's head. "What was the spray?"

"It is an antiseptic but has numbing in it as well." Rayne looked at Boon who sat enjoying the petting Jace was giving him with his tongue hanging out. "We'll get you fixed up."

She used her water bottle to pour some water over it and clean it up. The white gauze pad was bloody and brown, but the paw was much cleaner and didn't look quite so terrible. Rayne knelt next to him spraying more of the analgesic to help desensitize it, added antibiotic ointment, and a fresh pad to cover and protect it, and wrapped the whole thing up with gauze and this time neon pink athletic tape.

"He's just going to rip it off again." Jace swatted Boon's attempt at chewing it minutes after she finished.

Rayne sat back on her heels glancing around. "Humm, something strong enough for these big chompers." She reached out and ruffled the fur between his ears. "Yet… Pliable enough to walk on."

A small secondhand boutique caught her eye. "I'll be right back."

She hurried to the store and cautiously went inside while Jace and Boon watched after her. Boon tugged to go after her, but Jace held his collar. "She'll be right back," he cooed at the dog. Moments later she emerged with a smile on her face.

She'd foraged a few items to protect the paw and emerged with her bounty in tow. A child's rain boot which was too big and slid right off. An oven mitt, which ended up a comical adventure Boon thought made a great chew toy and finally the boot for a golf club. "Here we go, you're number one buddy."

Jace helped her stretch the upper part over the injured paw and slid the bootie over the whole thing. The bottom end was fake leather and slightly large but the neck of it was stretchy and tight. They hoped it would keep it in place. Rayne wrapped another round of tape on the outside to keep it from flapping, smiled and reached out for another stroke down the dog's back.

"Sorry pal, not ripping it off today."

Boon slapped a wet, sloppy kiss right on her cheek and returned to panting, looking at both of them before the task of chewing the cover off his foot took his attention.

"He will just chew it off again," Jace sighed.

Rayne stood and pulled four more from her pocket. "We still have two, three, five, and six to go." She grinned at him. She'd grabbed other things as well. A pocketknife, old canteen, two warm coats, the putter from the golf set, and a small garden wagon.

"Why did you grab all that random stuff?" Jace looked at the small cart, eyeing it critically. "Heavy coats? It's August and hot as shit."

"I didn't know what kind of shape things would be in. If we need to get Kelly and go someplace, I wanted to make sure being pregnant and all, we could make her comfortable. Plus, even if not... I am tired of the hard ground. But the stuffing in the coats could filter water or be used to start fires. The outer layer is good rain gear. I thought of a stroller just in case but then figured the wagon was better with a newborn if we needed it. Hell, I don't know, I just grabbed some shit."

"And the golf club?"

"Ever get hit with a putter?" She eyed him squinting.

"Good point. Let's get going."

They hurried the last few blocks, the boot on Boon's foot slapping the ground with each step he tried to take. He limped mostly holding it up, but the foreign feel of the boot made his stride awkward. Some of the houses were flattened by the quakes, others burning. The houses left standing and mostly undamaged were few and far between. Jace's hopes of finding Kelly safe and sound at home were dwindling with each passing house. The neighborhood in rubble, they reached his street where he stopped dead in his tracks. His home was flattened, a pile of glass and debris and snapped off boards jutting out from the wreckage. He fell to his knees and put his hands to his head, entwining his hair and ripping at it.

"Dammit Jace!" Rayne's voice rose to a near panicked shriek. "Get up, let's get over there."

"But it's…" He trailed off.

"Seriously? We come all this way, and you just stare at it? What if she is inside? I said… Get up!"

Rayne grabbed his arm jerking at it, tugging him back to his feet. They ran the half a block to his home circling it, looking for a way in.

"Kelly!" He gasped ripping at boards and debris. "Kelly, are you here? C'mon, baby, where are you?" Sobs wracked his body as he ripped through the debris, frantically trying to get inside.

Boon circled the other end of the house whining. A single bark caught Rayne's attention and she tugged on Jace's shirt. "C'mon, Boon's found something."

Jace's face went ashen, all color draining from it when he saw the pile of rubble in the area Boon scratched.

Rayne cried out, "Help me!" as she tore at the debris.

She was trying to lift a large beam, part of the roof rafters. It was snapped off with only plywood and a few shingles still attached. Jace couldn't think, his mind fixated on the fate of his unborn child.

Finally, a moan from beneath some smaller bits spurred him to action. Ripping into it, flinging debris out behind him, he reached the source of it. He stood momentarily shocked when Rayne pulled a piece of insulation off of the man. She bent down and the man choked. Blood oozing from the corner of his mouth.

He croaked, "Jace, man… Where were you?"

"I was… Where's Kelly?" He knelt beside the man then looked to Rayne who slowly shook her head, nodding to the long splinter of wood jutting out of his abdomen.

She held Boon off to the side of the house, while Jace sat with his friend. It wasn't long before the man faded into unconsciousness and finally stopped breathing.

Jace continued to kneel beside him sobbing. "I can't do this." His hands on his head, he cursed, stood and began pacing in circles angrily. "My mother is right; I can't do anyone any good. Couldn't save Ian, couldn't save Noah over there… Why am I even alive?"

Rayne approached and placed a hand on his shoulder. He swatted it away, "Just go away…I'm no good to anyone."

Rayne's anger cut through his self-pity with her

biting words. "Wise up asshole and quit with the pity party. Kelly is not here; this is a good thing. Get your shit together and quit wallowing."

His eyes widened in anger as he turned to her. Fury etched his brow and he stepped toward her. "Why are you even here?" The venom in his voice meant to frighten her.

She stood resolved, "Because I promised to help you find her, because you saved me… You saved me and Boon. Quit yelling at me, I'm just trying to help you. How about this? I don't even know why I bothered." She tossed a small diaper bag to the ground in front of him that she'd pulled from the back end of the house. "Fuck off Jace." She flipped him the bird and turned to leave.

Jace stared at the bag they'd packed for the baby to go to the hospital, and tears burst from his already red and swollen eyes. "Rayne, wait…" He hoisted the bag and clutched it to his chest, walking to where she stood.

Her back to him and arms crossed, she humpfed, and refused to look at him.

"I'm sorry Rayne. I know you are just trying to help, and I am grateful. I didn't mean to…" His voice trailed off and he squeezed the diaper bag.

"Didn't mean to what? Be an asshole?"

"Yeah. It's just… I don't know what to do. I was sure she was here."

"Well, she's not," Rayne snapped. "And that is not a bad thing. Look around Jace, the house is gone." He looked up at her and she continued her voice softer, "Listen, Boon and me? We got no one here. You're stuck with us, just like we are stuck with you. I don't know what this bullshit about your mom is all about but neither of us would be here if it were not for you. Quit letting the demons of your past rule the future and let's go get Kelly."

"She said my dad left because of me. He never wanted children. Told me when I was little that I ruined her life. I could never be good enough; I didn't want that for my child." He confided his deep-seated fears of failure to her as they rummaged through the debris for things they thought they might need.

"Did you know I got into MIT? She said it would ruin her to have to pay the tuition, so I didn't go. I came out here to find a new life and was actually going to take a job in Wyoming with an oil company to give my family a good life. I found some stuff on the dark web about what they were doing that was not exactly ethical. So much has happened, I just don't know which end is up."

"Yeah, I get the family stuff. Someone once said, 'Childhood is something we spend the rest of our lives trying to get over'." Her lip raised slightly on one side into a crooked smile. "Cam, my sister? She was the perfect child; I was here trying to do the college thing. The new life as you say."

"Cam?" Jace asked, reaching for what was left of the refrigerator.

"Camilla, that's my sister. They are in Denver.

Remember the call? I don't think this is local but something much bigger. I think we should get Kelly and go east toward Denver. My dad has some things, and it is probably better than here."

"Look!" Jace exclaimed, pulling a small vial from the partially opened refrigerator. "Kelly's insulin."

Rayne dove into the refrigerator and jerked on the freezer door. "This is great, she may need it when we find her."

She pulled out a few packs of frozen vegetables and even found a couple of still frozen water bottles. She handed them to Jace, "Here, pack it in this."

The sun dipped low on the horizon as they packed things into the small wagon Rayne had found, the journey to Kelly's work on their minds. It was deeper into the city, moving toward Los Angeles into the heart of Pasadena. Jace worried it would take another twenty-four hours to reach her, but they would try. Rayne and Boon walked beside him as they made their way out of the subdivision.

"I'm coming, Kelly," he whispered to himself.

TWELVE

CAMI & THEO

Theo sat in the passenger seat brooding. Women were a complete mystery to him. Here he was defending her from that jerk off and now she's mad at him. He made note of his name, he'd see to it that he didn't have a job once all of this got back to normal.

Cami glanced hesitantly at Theo, who sat quietly looking out the window, his face pinched and brow low. She'd just reacted without thinking. What Rob had said was not so much true as it was hateful. He'd asked her out once, but it was only to get to Blythe. When Cami canceled the date after finding out that he wanted her to bring Blythe and that was the only reason he'd asked her, he became hostile toward her at work.

Theo had no way of knowing any of this, having literally been at work for little over an hour before all hell broke loose and he'd inadvertently stepped into a wasp's nest with all of this ongoing animosity. He sat stoically looking out the window considering what had just happened and whispered to himself that it would end when things got back to normal. Rob was history, no matter what Cami said about it.

He turned to her and took a deep breath. "Listen Cami...I'm uhh...I'm—"

Without looking at him she sighed. "Don't worry about it. I overreacted, there is a history there and he's just an asshole." She looked at him out of the corner of her eye. "I should be grateful, but for some reason I felt like I had to defend the fact that I was not sleeping with the boss even more after you gave him what he deserved."

Theo grinned slightly playfully, he really liked her and found her completely intriguing. "Well, you know we could..."

Her eyes flashed at him in horror as though he'd committed some horrific crime and he laughed.

"Oh, don't worry, I was just kidding."

Her face changed to something between confusion and indignation and suddenly he felt flushed.

"I mean not that I wouldn't want... But I was... Um... You're really... Well, I'm just gonna shut up now."

Cami laughed a real laugh, finding his discomfort hilarious. "It's ok, Mr. Teddy Three," she quipped. "How about we check the bump-and-dent store?"

"What's a bump-and-dent store?"

"You know the stores where they send the stuff that isn't perfect, and you can get it cheaper? There is one right up the road and I bet everyone is at the big stores now. Maybe we can find some things."

"Sounds good, but we need to make sure to get the non-food things on your dad's list. He was adamant that I make sure we got them."

"Ok well, there is a Home Depot just down here," she pointed ahead and to the right. "Then we can circle back and check the pharmacy while in the lot. There is a CVS next door to it."

His confidence returning, he sat straighter. He wished he'd met this woman outside of this mess. She was nothing like the girls he'd normally date. His father was all about power and looks pushing him at women who were—basically like Blythe. All looks, no brains. Or the power chick that he was forever in competition with. Cami's relaxed demeanor tugged at his gut. He chanced a look at her as she drove, her gentle eyes focused on the road ahead. A simple ponytail held her silky long hair behind her, with soft wisps in her eyes. She was beautiful. None of that overdone makeup, too much hairspray, or pretentious clothing. Just honest and lovely. Butterflies formed in his stomach and suddenly an awkward feeling of not knowing what to say choked his throat.

"Sounds like a plan." Was the best that he could muster sitting in his enamored state beside her.

She looked at him and smiled. "Thank you."

"For what?"

"Defending my honor."

He nodded at her, he wanted to defend her, to protect her, to know more about this woman. The woman his father would never approve of, yet she'd captured his attention completely.

They'd found things her dad wanted. Nails, tape, propane canisters for the small grill, two tarps, and some tools. The store had a generator and even the ATM worked. Theo immediately pulled cash from each of his cards. Cami was stunned at the stack of twenty-dollar bills in his hand.

"Did you empty the machine?"

He was shoving different amounts into different pockets and paused. "Uh… Yes."

She snorted a 'how did I guess' laugh and smirked at him. "I was actually kidding."

He readily paid for all the items and loaded them onto a flat cart to be packed into the Jeep. "I just thought we might need the cash and figured who knows when there will be another chance." He suddenly felt the need to explain.

"Oh, I agree," she sighed. "It's just that I am not used to seeing people who can just pull that much cash out of an ATM."

"Should I not have?" His confusion mounted; she

perplexed him at every turn.

"Oh… It is fine! I was just shocked." She winked at him and smiled warmly.

Once loaded, they headed for the last store. This would be all food items then a run to the pharmacy. They could not fit much more into the jeep. In the parking lot Cami insisted they each go to a different store to quicken the pace. He didn't like that idea, but reluctantly agreed. She went for the food while he hit the pharmacy. She'd be the one to get nonperishable food and promised to only be there for ten minutes. His job was first aid and whatever else the pharmacy would yield. He managed to get not only a whole bag of first aid items, but another also filled with over the counter drugs, as well as some pain medication and antibiotics he negotiated by paying off the pharmacist. Cold hard cash definitely has its purposes.

He sat outside the bump-and-dent store waiting for her and keeping watch on the Jeep when his phone rang again. It shocked him momentarily and he jumped, patting at his pockets to find the phone. Digging deep into his jacket pocket and pulling it out, he mashed the button to answer it.

"Dad?"

He listened to the call. His father was yelling at him this time. He couldn't understand what he was saying and put it on speaker. "Dad, slow down. What did you say?"

"Your grandmother is dead. She had a heart attack with the last quake. She was all alone, Theodore. This is your fault! You should have been here instead of traipsing off across the country."

"But, Dad," he pleaded. "It was a good job offer."

Cami came out of the store and heard Theo pleading with his father.

"You belong in our company. I'm disappointed in you. As usual."

Theo tried to talk to him, but he continued to berate him, eventually he just stood there listening quietly as his father's tirade went on. Cami backed into the doorway of the store so that he would not see her and be embarrassed.

The line went dead and Theo sat on the bench outside with the phone in his hands hanging down between his knees. Staring off into the parking lot he mumbled, "A disappointment."

Cami emerged from the doorway as though just exiting the store. "I got lots of stuff and even these." She held up a box of Ho-Ho's grinning widely.

Theo let out an uneasy laugh and smiled at her. "Oh, well, that will fix nearly everything, you know."

"Of course, they will." She ripped open the box as he loaded the items into the back seat, handing him a packet when he climbed into the vehicle.

He took it and smiled at her, peeling the package and shoving a whole one into his mouth as she bit hers. "So, time to head back?" His voice muffled from the mouthful.

"Actually, I was thinking about the camping store. What about if we look for some camping gear just in case we have to evacuate or anything."

He nodded, shoving the second cake into his mouth. "Good thinking, is it far?"

"No, it is on the way back if we go around the block."

"Well, then drive on my lady."

Inside the camping store, the clerk had already started price gouging. A tent was four hundred fifty dollars and a lantern two hundred. Everything was marked up a thousand percent. Theo was angry and pulled Cami aside. "Do we need this?"

"I don't know, what do you think?"

"I think this guy is a piece of shit and I should smack the shit outta him but that won't help. I don't want to waste what we have for cash. I have enough but if we spend it all here, we won't have it when we need it. Let me see if he will take a credit card."

Theo tried to sound as businesslike as possible when approaching the man who was dickering over some ammunition with another guy. "Excuse me?"

The clerk looked at him and moved to engage him as the other man would not leave and he looked to be glad for the diversion. "How can I help you?"

"You do know that price gouging is illegal, right?"

The man's face grew red instantly. "Get out, get out

now."

"Hold it now, I want to cut a deal with you." Theo's voice went deeper. "I get it, the law of supply and demand, right? We just have a cart of camping equipment. I want to offer you a bit more to take my credit card."

"The card machines aren't working. It's cash or nothing." The man sneered at him ignoring the angry guy he'd been talking to.

"Listen, I will give you the card and a signed permission to charge it when the power returns, along with an agreement not to sue you for this illegal price gouging."

The clerk sneered at him and squinted his eyes. "Or... You can pay cash and prove it later."

Theo raised his hands and turned to Cami, who responded with a no. They'd already decided if need be, they would just check another store. The angry man smashed the case where the ammo was and began grabbing boxes of bullets. The clerk ran to stop him, and the man fired, striking him in the chest. He crumpled to his knees, his eyes wide, a red spot growing on his green shirt.

Theo looked at Cami, grabbed an armload of ammo, and threw it into the cart. He reached for her, gripping her hand, shoving her and the cart to the door. He led her to the passenger door, motioned her inside and threw the items into the back of the Jeep. He had no idea where they were, and Cami was still staring at the entrance to the store. Starting the Jeep, he yelled to get her attention. "Which way?"

THIRTEEN

JACE

They walked through the night and like the one before, looters, fires, and gunshots rocked the streets. Jace put the leash on Boon to keep him close and Rayne found herself often gripping his arm. Fearful of the chaos surrounding them, her eyes darted into every dark corner searching for warning or attack. They kept to the smaller streets and alleys to avoid the gangs that either already existed and simply took over, or the newly formed gangs of roving looters seeking to profit from the disaster.

Jace guessed it was about three in the morning and they were all exhausted, even Boon limped along slowly. A van parked beside a dumpster in the alley looked like a good place to grab a few winks of sleep. The doors were unlocked, and windows tinted that allowed some feeling of safety. They climbed in and while Jace tried to take the first watch Rayne insisted he sleep at least for an hour and then she could grab some sleep. Her reasoning being that he'd suffered emotional trauma and needed to be on the ball tomorrow when they found Kelly. She would need him to be strong.

"I'll just sit up front and keep an eye on the mirrors." She clamored over the seat and stretched in the passenger side. Her eye caught a small green LED light glowing in the dark.

"Shit! A phone charger that works." She snatched up the cord and it was for an android phone. "It figures." She tossed the cord on the floor.

Jace reached into his pack and pulled out a small plug for a USB charger and passed it to her. "Do you have a cord?"

She fished through her things and the white cord emerged like a long snake. She squealed with excitement and set to plugging in her phone, leaned back and gazed out the mirrors for any movement.

Jace's eyelids were heavy, he hadn't slept since the small store and sleep washed over him in mere moments.

Music shattered the silence in the small space and both of them bolted upright. The sun was up. Rayne had fallen asleep as well and they both slept for some hours. The same number that had called before was calling again and Rayne fumbled with the screen lock to answer the call.

She quickly put it to her ear. "Hello... Hello... Cam? Is that you?"

A voice on the other end that Jace could not hear screeched. "What? Wait a minute, let me put you on speaker."

Rayne put the call on speaker and a female voice excitedly emerged. "Oh, Rayne, I'm so glad I reached you. Something has happened in Denver, but Dad, Joey and I are all fine."

"Denver?" Rayne questioned and paused. "Did the quakes reach all the way to Denver?"

Cami was silent for a few moments, some mumbling in the background filtered through before she continued. "No Ray it is something else. Near as we can tell it is all over the country. A guy on the radio was talking from West Virginia and they are having quakes too. Are you ok?"

Jace hung over the back of the seat and tears flowed down Rayne's cheeks. "Cam we are ok, but I don't know what to do. I'm scared, Cam. Really scared."

A strong voice chimed in on the conversation as Jace listened and took it all in. "Ray, it's ok honey. You're ok and that is all that matters right now. We will get this figured out."

"Daddy?"

"Yeah, honey. It's dad and we're all fine."

"Listen Ray, save this number, it's a satellite phone that belongs to my boss. The volcano has knocked out our cell coverage but this one will get through. You need to come home, Ray. Can you find a car or something and get here?"

"I'll try. But first we need to find Kelly."

"Who is Kelly?"

"She is Jace's pregnant girlfriend. I wouldn't be here right now if it were not for him. Cam… He saved my life."

"Thank him for us, we are so glad you have him. Bring them with you but come home, Rayne. Come home!"

Rayne looked at Jace who hung on the back of the seat and nodded to him. He offered a slight smile and began to gather his things.

"Ok, Cam. We are headed out; I will call later on if I can." She pressed the red button to end the call and tears poured down her cheeks. She sobbed into her hands, immobile and unable to think.

Jace reached for her. "We slept too late. We need to get moving so we can get to Kelly and get the hell outta here. You heard your sister; we need to get you home."

She looked up at him, her tear-streaked face and red eyes questioning. "Really?"

Jace had no idea if they would actually get to Denver or even if it was safe to try, but he knew one thing: he needed Rayne just as much as she needed him if they were going to find Kelly and survive this. "Sure, let's get going."

Initially, his only goal was to get her to a hospital or authority. Shake off the baggage of an extra person, find Kelly and keep her safe. The sudden realization that he was so wrong about everything consumed his thoughts. How could he keep her safe? What about the baby? If this is all over, then what's next?

Somewhere between the question of what was next and how he was going to do it, another even stronger quake rocked the area. Buildings swayed and debris fell from the tops of them. Jace grabbed Rayne's arm and Boon's leash and jerked them into an open parking lot ducking between two cars. Rayne screamed wildly, her head in her hands, while car alarms sounded, and debris peppered the area. On the next block a tall building leaned, Jace could see it reaching for its neighbor. The violent shaking continued for what to them felt like an eternity. Rayne began to vomit, retching, hunched over on her hands and knees from the swaying motion of the ground.

A loud crunching and screeching shattered their ears and both reached up to cover them. Boon howled in fear and pain from the sound. The building let go, its base crumbling. Screams barely audible from windows with people hanging out, some leaping to their death. Jace grabbed Boon around the neck and Rayne by the arm, pulling them closer, huddling beside the car, waiting for it to end.

Minutes later the shaking stopped, but like before, not entirely. A small trembling buzzed beneath them like a motor running. Jace stood first, looking around. Behind him a gas line exploded, the percussion knocking him on top of Rayne. Again, she screamed, in near hysterics clawing at the ground to get out from under him.

Jace grabbed her, pulling her back and shouted. "Rayne! Grab your gear. We need to go."

It took a moment for her to gather herself, but she stood, slinging her pack onto her shoulders ready to move. She nodded to him. "I'm ready. Sorry. I just really hate earthquakes."

They began to navigate the broken city blocks, fires and debris surrounding them until they reached the place that Kelly worked. Two days had passed and hopes of finding her there were waning.

Jace burst through the door of the small boutique calling out her name. "Kelly," he screamed. "Kelly, are you here?"

A small man emerged from the back room carrying a long ornamental sword. "Get out, leave," he shouted and held the heavy sword before him, barely able to keep the tip of it off the ground.

Jace raised his hands to be non-threatening. "Listen, I am just looking for Kelly. She works here."

"Oh, her," the man scoffed. "She ran off the first day. Her and that other worthless clerk went to the hospital. Something about the baby and insulin." He turned and put the sword on the counter, the tinny sound clanking. "I should have known better than to keep a pregnant woman on, they always run out, you know. Have the kid and never come back." He went on grumbling behind the counter.

Boon growled and the man looked surprised. "Get that mangy thing out of my store. There are no dogs allowed in here." He began waving his hands shooing them out the door.

Jace's anger was welling up inside him, he wanted to grab that fake sword and smack the shit out of this little twerp. Rayne reached for his arm pulling him back toward the door.

"Thank you for the information. Let's go, Jace."

Once outside Rayne was excited but Jace looked injured. "What's wrong? This is a good thing," she exclaimed.

"She's not here. We still haven't found her."

"Yes but, your worries about the insulin Jace... Think about it, if she went to the hospital, they would have what she needs. At least we know she is safe, all we gotta do is go find her."

His head raised and he peered past her toward the direction of the hospital. "It's only about a mile up the road." He pointed in the direction of it.

"Ok then, what are we waiting for? Let's go!"

They walked right up the road dodging the cars and cracks in the road. The mile took more than an hour, but the excitement grew with each step he took. He began to talk of things he wanted to do with his child. "Did I tell you it's a boy?" He looked at Rayne with a real smile.

"You didn't," she grinned back. "Did you think of a name?"

"Yeah, Kelly wanted to name him after me, but I want something else, something more important."

Rayne frowned at him. "What is wrong with Jace?"

"That's just a nickname. Jason Ryan Walker, at your service." He bowed.

"I can see why she liked it. Definite possibilities," her eyes gazing skyward, she tapped her temple. "Lots of nicknames for him, Jace of course."

Jace scrunched his nose and shook his head.

"Jason, Ryan? How about J.R.? Think about it J.R. Walker… Jr."

He waved her off and pointed to the large building looming ahead of them. "There it is. Let's go." He skipped and began to jog toward the emergency room entrance.

Just as they got within a few feet of the door it smashed. Shards of glass flying outward at them. Jace ducked but Rayne got sprayed with slivers of glass. Small cuts on her face and hands begin to trickle tiny drops of blood immediately. Six or eight people staggered out of the shattered door hooting and smashing vials and containers of medicine and blood onto the ground. One stopped, pouring a bottle of pills down his throat, and washing it down with a long pull of Jack Daniels. He spotted Jace and threw the empty bottle at his head. His face twisting into a demented rage, he screamed and lunged at him.

Rayne ducked behind a large SUV and Jace made for a car that sat on its side, skirting around behind it. The gang of drugged up looters slammed into the bottom of the car pushing it over on top of Jace. His leg was caught under the roof and pinned to the ground, he was stuck. In a panic, his fingers clawed away at the dirt, digging at the ground to release him. The drugged-up looters taunted him, kicking him and throwing things at him until darkness surrounded his vision and the world went dark. Weakly gasping, "Kelly—"

FOURTEEN

THEO

Theo's turns were erratic as he drove to get back to Cami's house, but the roads were mired with debris and stalled cars from the ash. Cami navigated, sending him up one street and down another. Pulling over he stopped to look at her. Tears streaked the gray dust on her face as she sat stoically looking forward out the windshield. It took a moment for her to realize they'd stopped. When she did, her look to Theo was a mask of fear and confusion.

"Are you ok?"

She shook her head and fresh tears followed the tracks to her chin. "I was so scared. What happened?"

"I'm sorry," he cooed and reached for her.

She jerked her hand away from him. "What the hell did we do?"

"Us?" he exclaimed. "We didn't do a damn thing. Well—except for swiping some over-priced camping equipment, we had nothing to do with it. We were just bystanders, but I didn't want us to be involved and ran for it."

She continued to look at him, horror settled deeply behind her eyes.

"You know... I can pay for it and if it makes you feel better, we can write down what happened with a list and a description of the guy and when this is all over report it and pay for the items."

Her eyebrows came together in the middle. "You mean if this is ever over?"

Theo sat back in the seat, rolled down the window and looked out the driver's side to hide his trepidation. "I don't know," his voice softer. "We may have to do things we never thought possible to survive in the future. But, for now I have to hope this will all blow over." He turned and looked at her. "Cami, I don't want you to think of me this way. I'm not... I mean, I find you... What I'm trying to say is, after everything gets back to normal, I hope you won't think of me as a bad guy. Maybe we could even go out?" He looked at her hopefully.

She snorted and laughed. "You're kidding right? Theodore James Brandywine the third, head of the entire Denver office wants to go out with Camilla James, Clerk."

"Why not?" His look changed to irritation.

"Because," she scoffed. "Guys like you want to go out with someone like Blythe. Arm candy that is willing to do anything to be hanging off the important guy's arm."

He shrugged; she was right. All of his past girlfriends were nothing but fluff, no brains, no ambition beyond hanging off his arm. Arm candy. Which is why he tired of them quickly. He looked at Cami, more intrigued than ever and elbowed her arm in a playful way.

"Well, now, isn't this interesting." The familiar voice boomed outside the window. "Getting all cozy with the boss man, are we?"

"Fuck! Not you again." Theo gasped and started to open the car door.

Rob Stearns slammed the door into him. "Sit tight, Pretty Boy. We wanna have a little chat with the lady here."

"Rob, go away." Cami warned him, "You will regret this when things get back to normal."

"There ain't gonna be no normal and whores like you are good for one thing in this here apopkeylips and we are gonna get that started right now, aren't we boys." He looked over his shoulder at two other guys. "First let's take care of Pretty Boy here."

Theo objected and reached to the center console for the gun Cami's dad had given him. Before he could retrieve it Rob yanked him from the Jeep and the other two hopped on top of him. They held him down as Rob began to kick him in the ribs.

Cami screamed, "Stop it! Stop it now! Why are you doing this?"

Rob paused his attack to spin on her. His words, biting and venomous. "This is all your fault. You let Blythe fall to get rid of her so you could have the pretty boy here all to yourself. You treated me like a piece of shit back at the grocery store thinking, you're all high and mighty now. But, you're not now are you?" he hissed at her.

"You're insane!" She backed away from the door as he leaned in, the stench of cigarettes and old whisky on his breath.

"You sit tight while we finish up with your boyfriend, we'll take care of you shortly." He turned and joined the frenzy of beating on Theo.

Blood running into his eye from the gash on his head, Theo was powerless as Rob leaned into the car after Cami, horrified at what they meant to do to her. He croaked out to her, "Cami, run."

"Fuck this," she growled. Flipping up the center console where the gun sat loaded. She grabbed it and pointed it out the driver's door, closed her eyes, and pulled the trigger.

BOOM!

The echo inside the jeep was thunderous. One of the men holding Theo dropped to the ground writhing and screaming. "The bitch shot me."

Rob turned to see her pointing the gun in his face. Her hand shaking, finger clenching on the trigger pulling it closer to firing a second time. "I'll do it!" she screamed. "Leave us alone!"

Rob backed away with his hands up. "Relax, don't do anything crazy."

"Crazy?" she screeched, her hand shaking, still slowly pulling on the trigger. "Are you fucking kidding me? *You're* calling *me* crazy? Screw you asshole. I'd be doing the world a favor." She closed her eyes and yanked it.

The boom happened and the bullet whizzed right past Rob's head. He stumbled backward, falling over Theo. The three men crawled past where Theo was laying, getting up and running down the street.

Rob called out, "You'll pay for this, bitch!"

Cami dropped the gun back into the center console and scrambled out of the Jeep, stumbling as she ran to Theo then helping him up and over to the passenger door. The pain in his ribs told him that they were likely broken. He coughed and fell to his knees, the sharp stabbing in his side nearly making him pass out.

"I'm sorry," he wheezed.

"Nonsense." She helped him into the seat and closed the door, running around the vehicle, to jump in the driver's side. Starting the vehicle and slamming it into gear she floored it and the Jeep lurched forward making Theo cry out in pain. "Hang on, we are only about half a mile from the house."

Horn blowing loudly as she pulled into the driveway, it was only moments before the garage door opened and she pulled it inside. She screamed at her father. "Help him."

Doug ran to the passenger side of the car and flung the door open. Theo's rapidly swelling eye was nearly shut but he tried to look at him, he coughed and winced in pain.

"Dammit, I was worried about this," Doug said as he reached in for Theo. He paused, his eyes going over Cami assessing if she was injured.

"Dad, please. Let's get him inside."

Joey stumbled out the door into the garage stunned at the activity surrounding the Jeep. "Can I help?"

Cami pointed to the door. "Hurry, close it."

Joey ran to the roll up door, leaped for the handle and pulled it down. Twisting the latch to secure it in place before hurrying over to where Cami was frantically offloading things from the back seat.

"Wow, what a haul!" Joey exclaimed.

"I need to find the bag from the pharmacy."

Joey rummaged on the passenger side while Cami pulled bags and items from the vehicle, placing them in a pile on the floor inside the garage.

"Ho-Ho's!" Joey exclaimed.

"C'mon, Joey, please focus. White bags with CVS on them."

"Oh, right here." He hoisted the bag full of first aid items.

"There is more, are they over there?"

"Yup, right here." He walked around the Jeep with the three bags in his hands and a round cake in his mouth. Handing them to her, he took the cake and bit down, smiling after her as she bolted for the door inside. "Don't worry, I got this." He waved her off.

Fifteen

Jace

Shards of light stung his eyes in flashes and the pain wracking his body instantly reminded him of what happened. A muffled voice called out to him, but he couldn't fully hear it. Then warm, wet slobber blanketed his cheek, and his vision began to return. The massive head of Boon, inches from his face, loomed in his vision and another slobbery swipe from the wet tongue washed across his face. Jace feebly reached for the dog who laid down beside him, a small whimper escaped before a high-pitched yelp.

Rayne's face came into view. Tears rolling freely, she shook him. "Jace... Oh my God, Jace, wake up."

Jace's head and back hurt where they'd kicked him, but he'd managed to protect most of the vital areas by curling himself up tight to the car. The worst was his head. Whoever kicked him in the head had hard boots, maybe steel toed.

"Jace!" Rayne exclaimed. "Oh, thank God, you're alive."

"Yeah. My head hurts like there is no tomorrow but I think I'm ok. What the hell happened?"

"They were like a crazed mob, it was insane. They rushed you and were in some kind of a frenzy," she sobbed. "I thought they were going to kill you, and just like that they stopped and went after a few people over there." She pointed to the far side of the hospital. "They went around the building. I don't know where they are now, but we gotta get out of here before they come back."

"I can't," Jace exclaimed. "My leg… It's stuck."

Rayne tried pulling on his leg. Then standing, tried to lift the car, it was futile. She started digging at the ground with her hands and frustration overwhelmed her. "I don't know what to do," she sobbed.

"Go… Try and find someone to help."

"I can't just leave you here."

"Boon will stay with me." He reached out for the dog who was mightily trying to dig at the ground where Rayne had been digging. "Right, boy?" Jace gripped his leash and nodded to her.

She stood to look around for someone to help and he touched her ankle.

"Rayne, hurry please?"

She nodded and hurried toward a small strip mall

across from the hospital. Jace held Boon's leash when he tried to follow after her, pulling the dog close and hugging his neck. "Thanks, buddy."

Jace was getting nervous, Rayne did not come back right away. He blew out a long breath and tried to quell the worry and began digging at the hard grass beneath him. Dirt rammed painfully under his fingernails with each clawing motion. He got Boon in on the digging and dirt flew out behind the dog, but unfortunately it was not from under his leg but beside it.

Boon stopped suddenly and barked. Jace turned to see Rayne running at him with an older man following closely.

"He's here," she said, panting as she approached.

"Well, young man, you seem to have gotten yourself in a pickle." The older man had a kind face and reached to shake his hand. "Let's get you out of here."

The man went around to the driver's side and pressed the trunk release. The trunk popped open with a few contents spilling to the ground. Moving to the back of the car, he began to rummage up inside the truck area emerging with the car's jack. A simple scissor jack and crooked rod.

"I should have thought of that," Jace cursed.

Rayne watched intently as the man set it near the back window, between it and the open trunk at the hinge. He began to crank the crooked rod and the scissors began to rise. "Missy, I need you to come over here and keep cranking this." I will try to lift the car to make it easier but it is not stable. We need to pull him out as soon as there is enough clearance."

Rayne hurried over to continue cranking while the man lifted on the rear door handle to assist the small jack in lifting the vehicle.

"I can feel it," Jace exclaimed. "I can wiggle my foot a little."

"Keep cranking." The man strained harder to lift on the vehicle. "Quickly, go help him pull the leg out." While he tried to steady the now teetering vehicle. "Hurry before the jack topples."

Rayne yanked on his pant leg while he pushed himself back. A few inches at a time his leg began to emerge.

"Hurry!" the man yelled.

Rayne grasped around his knee and jerked with all she had. The leg popped out from under the roof of the car, and they went flying backward onto the grass just as the jack toppled over shifting the car and slamming it back into the ground.

The man slumped, releasing the tension in his back and arms. "Are you ok, young man?"

"I think so."

"Can you walk?"

Jace struggled to get up, between the numbness in his leg from being pinned and the bad ankle he already had, he looked like a marionette who's strings had been tangled.

Once righting himself he twisted the ankle and stretched the leg. It was uninjured other than some bruises.

"Thank you," Jace offered his hand. "We have to get into the hospital. My girlfriend is there."

"I came here looking for blood pressure medication myself. My wife needs it and hers was lost in the quake." The man nodded toward the shattered doors. "I've been trying to get in but these drug heads have had it overrun. It's like they've moved in. My wife is in our car on the next block. I didn't want her near this."

"Well, I think they all took off." Rayne looked from one to the other hopeful. "Maybe we can get in now."

"Let's go." Jace nodded to both of them and took a step toward the door.

Before they could go another foot, five people staggered out the door, and ducked down behind another car. A woman stopped mid stride and projectile vomited on one of them. He shoved her to the ground, and they continued to run from the building. Standing behind the car they watch the woman begin to convulse on the pavement in front of the entrance. No one emerged to help her and Jace began to walk in her direction.

The man grabbed his arm. "Hold on. Something is wrong."

"What? What do you mean?"

"Why is no one coming out of the hospital to help her?"

Jace jerked his arm from the man's grip. "I don't care." His voice was angry. "I need to get inside. Kelly's in there."

Jace turned for the door and took two steps, glancing back to shoot a dirty look at the man and Rayne. A low hissing sound grew louder coming from the ER doors. Before he could register what was happening, the explosion knocked him to the ground, glass blowing out of all the lower windows in the hospital. The ground shuddered and Jace scrambled back to them. More smaller explosions climbed the floors in different areas as the ignition continued.

"What the fuck?" Jace screamed, holding his ears.

The man reached out to steady Jace, whose knees gave out as he sank to the ground. "I think it may be the oxygen. They have large tanks in the basement of the building feeding to the rest of the hospital. We need to run!"

Rayne yanked Jace's arm, and the man latched onto the other, as well as Boon's leash. "Run, dammit!"

The percussion from the bigger blast sent projectiles flying in every direction. A large chunk of metal exploded through the old man's chest from behind impaling him. His lifeless body slumped to the ground dragging Jace with him. Rayne's screaming pierced the air unheard beside the rumble of the raging inferno behind them. The scene was ghastly; two burning bodies of those trying to escape writhed near where they once stood. The sky rained chunks of cement, metal, and various charred remains of the occupants of the building.

Jace's mind couldn't wrap itself around what had just happened. He stood in a silent stupor, glancing from body to body, refusing to accept that Kelly would be dead. Boon barked and yelped wildly, trying to escape the leash the man still had firmly wrapped around his wrist, dragging him inches at a time as Boon jerked himself away from the flaming building. The man's arm stretched behind the dog, metal pole through his chest digging into the ground keeping Boon from dragging him or escaping.

SIXTEEN

THEO

Theo slept; the pain medication Doug had given him did a good job of knocking him out. Waking, he recalled every blow, highlighted by the pain emanating from every part of his body. He groaned when rolling onto his side and immediately felt sick.

Cami sat by the bed and pushed a trash can closer for him to throw up in. His pride crushed as he vomited into the can. Cami's warm hand gently rested on his back and somehow it didn't feel so bad. The soothing voice seemed to calm the spasms in his gut. He rolled onto his back and lay spent, looking at her.

"Some hero I turned out to be."

She smiled softly at him and stood. "I'm going to get you some broth, it's been a while and you could use the nutrients. Dad wanted to talk to you when you woke up."

Her soft hand reached for his and an electric charge seemed to flow up his arm when she touched him.

In the past all Theo had to do was drive up in his flashy car, or generously tip a waiter, for women to think he was the cat's meow and be all over him. That is, besides the ones who knew who he was and pursued him relentlessly for the money. He was tall with dark shoulder length hair that he let fall across one side of his face in dramatic fashion for effect. But this one… She knew who he was and yet refused to fall under his spell. He was fascinated with this. He considered everything since the minute he laid eyes on her.

Sure, Blythe was his typical arm candy. But Cami, she excused herself, letting her friend fawn all over him. Even in that first moment he felt compelled to pursue her into the outer office, curious at this woman who did not fall at his feet. "Teddy Three," he whispered and softly laughed to himself. He relaxed his body and lay back with a slight smile.

Cami returned with her dad and some warm broth. Sitting up was a struggle, his ribs hurt so bad. She carefully propped some extra pillows behind his back and handed him the warm liquid. The salty hot broth soothed his raw throat and felt wonderful in his empty stomach. Immediately, his spirits raised, and he felt more alert.

Doug stood over him with a curious look on his face. "Nice to see you still with us."

"Why? Was I…? I mean, is it bad? Am I hurt badly?" He began to reach for his chest and head looking for some fatal wound he was unaware of. Patting himself down, the anxiety rising.

Doug laughed, "No, no, you're going to be ok. I don't even think your ribs are broken. Bruised, maybe even cracked, but I didn't feel anything out of place. This is a good thing."

"Oh man, you scared me there for a minute." Theo grimaced when he tried to sit straighter. "Is everything ok? Cami said you wanted to talk to me."

"Yes, I did." Doug looked at Cami. "Can you excuse us for a moment, honey?"

Cami squinted her eyes at her father suspiciously and flashed him a warning look before grabbing the cup and leaving the room.

"I just wanted to thank you for looking out for Cam," Doug sighed.

"I… Uh…" Theo had no idea what to say, Cami saved his ass. As a matter of fact, he was feeling pretty damn useless in all of this.

"Oh, I know she fired the gun at those assholes but if you hadn't been there to begin with…" His hand went to his forehead. "I can't even speak what I fear."

Theo didn't say anything and just listened to the distraught man. He could see that he was unraveling, full of worry and anxiety. But what had changed since they got back to change his perspective?

"Is everything ok, sir… Uh, I mean Doug?"

"I don't believe so." Doug looked relieved that he'd asked. "Cami told me she spoke to Rayne and things are terrible out west."

"Yes, but my father spoke of the quakes that first night. Is there a reason why now you are so concerned?"

"Well, I kind of figured that these quakes were tectonic, even though the volcano woke up, and didn't really think much of it. Los Angeles gets quakes all the time. It just made sense. But I heard a broadcast while you two were gone, some guy with a ham radio passed on information from others around the world. There were so many reports that after a while I didn't even hear them any more. I couldn't stop thinking about the kids."

Theo just stared blankly at him.

"Did you hear me?" Doug asked, tapping his shoulder. "I said the world is falling apart."

Theo's eyes slowly moved to meet Doug's. "We need a plan."

"What?"

"A plan, we need to know what is going on. Where things are happening, and get Cami to safety."

Doug looked at him, brows furrowed accusingly.

"I mean Cami and Joey. But more than that, when we spoke to Rayne she planned to come here. I'm sorry, my mind is still a little foggy." He reached for his head feeling the ooze of blood that was partially dried and sticking to his hair. "Sir, I know you don't know me, but Cami saved me not once but multiple times. I know no one here and my father? Well, let's just say I envy Cami and Joey." He hung his head and continued, "I had no intentions of returning to California even if it were safe."

Doug sat nodding at him without a word.

"I don't mind saying I've never met a woman like Cami before and I plan to spend some time getting to know her."

Doug's eyes narrowed and Theo put his hands up.

"Completely honorable, I promise."

"Well, this is not the kind of information I'd hoped to discuss with you but I'm glad you were honest. Does Cami know?"

"Ummm… No. She gets mad at me every time I try to do some manly, chivalrous thing. I have no clue what the hell I'm doing."

Doug laughed and patted his shoulder again. "Welcome to the club son, no man has a clue what to do with women."

Theo nodded, feeling a bit disarmed and self-conscious. "I guess."

"So," Doug began, changing the subject. "This plan? What are you thinking?"

"I don't really know, but we do know your other daughter plans to come here. Do you think we can shelter in place for now? Can we make this place at least somewhat safe?"

"This is what I didn't tell Cami," Doug's eyes pierced his. "The reports said that small eruptions have begun at Yellowstone. Do you know what that means?"

"Not really, I know it is a big volcano, but it is all the way up in Wyoming."

"Yellowstone is a super volcano, this means that the ashfall, if it really goes, will come here. If we wait, we may not be able to get out from under it, but if we go… How will Rayne find us?

"Did she say for sure she was coming here?" Doug leaned in expectantly.

"Yeah, I think that was what the plan was. You'd have to talk to Cami, she is the one that spoke with her. I think we need to include her in how we decide things. I know you don't want to alarm her, but between what you know and what Rayne told her we might be able to get a clearer picture of things. All I know is Rayne was looking for the girlfriend of this guy that was with her. We can try calling her again, I really don't know how long the cell towers will last and the key is that she has to be near one that is working. Whatever the plan is, I think it is important that we include Cami and Joey."

"Joey is just a kid," Doug scoffed.

Theo raised himself partially from the pillow and grunted. "He's a smart kid and thinks on his feet."

"Whoa… Whoa… Whoa… Where do you think you're going?" Doug hopped up to move toward Theo.

"I really don't want to lay here." He grimaced, shifting his weight to swing his legs off the bed. "I don't think we should waste time. I want to join the others and besides, I don't want Cami mad at me for excluding her." He snorted a small laugh and then coughed, grasping his side.

Doug reached out to help him up. Theo was nearly half-standing when Cami came back, startling them. Theo gripped Doug around the neck, the two of them staring at her like the cat that just ate the canary.

Cami stood in the doorway looking at them with her hands on her hips. "What the hell are you doing?"

"We, ahh…." Doug Stammered.

"I'm trying to … Well, umm…" Theo felt like a child being scolded for having his hand in the cookie jar.

"He can't be up." Cami hurried to his side, glaring at her father. "He needs to rest."

Theo reached for her hand and gave her a crooked smile. "Help me, please? I want to go into the other room. We wanted to chat with you and Joey about what's going on."

"It can wait," she said, trying to get her father to put him back in the bed.

"No, Camilla, it can't"

The sharp bite to her dad's voice shocked her. She halted what she was doing and turned to him. "Why not?"

"I'm fine, Cami." Theo's hand brushed hers and she looked down at it and then up into his eyes. "I would feel better if I could just prop up on the sofa with everyone else. Please?"

Her lips pursed and she climbed up under his other arm, helping to steady him. "Thank you," he whispered into her hair.

"Humph," Cami grunted.

SEVENTEEN

JACE

The percussion from the explosion stunned them for a few moments. Rayne crawled for the body of the man who'd helped them to retrieve Boon's leash, while Jace's wide eyes stared at the inferno, unable to move, deaf to her cries for him to follow. He couldn't believe Kelly was dead...his son. He'd promised to be the father he always wanted and failed. He couldn't save them. His head fell into his hands as despair took over and immobilized him. But still Jace sat motionless, his left side splattered in blood from the man who'd helped them, the muffled cries for help coming from the hospital like a nightmare. He couldn't move, lost in his agony.

Rayne tugged at his arm but he barely registered it until a low rumble began to shake the area again. At first it could be barely felt. A water bottle lay a few feet from him and the water inside rippled with the vibration. He stared at it curiously watching the liquid as the shaking became more violent, jostling it until the bottle finally rolled into the street and Rayne shook him from his stupor.

"What the hell are you doing?" Her voice was suddenly loud, screaming at him.

"Wha?" Jace looked up at her, still in shock.

"Move it!" she screamed, yanking at his arm.

All at once he was on his feet. Someone much stronger than Rayne had hoisted him from the ground. He turned and a big man wearing a leather vest stood on the opposite side of him.

"Let's go, buddy," the gruff voice of the man commanded.

Rayne looked at the man gratefully and grabbed Jace's arm dragging him across the street. They took cover in the park kitty corner from the hospital as the quake rolled over the area. The front entrance to the hospital crumpled and caved in, burying people inside but the emergency entrance still stood. People continued to stagger out of the building, some helping the injured.

The quake subsided and Jace bolted for the hospital but didn't make it far as the large man halted him. "Wait, it's not done."

"But I need to…" Jace protested.

"We all do," the man chided. "But killing ourselves won't do any good for those we hope to help." His voice was softer, and he nodded at Jace. "I need to get in there and find my sister, she's a nurse." His eyes fell to the ground.

It wasn't long before the quake stopped and the three of them moved toward the entrance. Boon whined and stood fast; he did not want to go. Rayne pulled on his leash, but the dog refused to move.

"Jace… Jace, it's Boon. He won't move," Rayne called after him.

He stopped and turned to look at them. "C'mon Boon." Jace slapped his leg. "Let's go boy."

Boon still refused to move.

"Let's go," the man urged. "Leave the dog, we need to go help them."

"You go," Jace scowled. "This dog has saved my life on more than one occasion; I'm not leaving him anywhere. We stick together."

The man huffed and turned to leave but stood rigid and fumed instead scanning the people who came out and waited.

Jace moved to Boon stroking his ears and down his back where the fur was raised. "What's wrong boy?" he cooed.

Boon whimpered and crouched low, crawling toward Jace. The ground shook violently, knocking all of them to their knees, unable to stand. The man's eyes widened, shooting a look at them before they all gazed at the hospital again.

The canopy over the entrance crashed to the ground and a full half of the building caved in upon itself on the far side. Jace cried out and crawled a few feet before collapsing into tears.

It finally ended, the trio and the dog headed for the chaos to find their loved ones. Jace cried out "Kelly!" Shouting into the opening to the ER. He reached into his pack and pulled out his wallet, handing Rayne a photo of her. "Please, help me find her."

They asked everyone they saw about the nurse or the pregnant woman. No one could help with a nurse, there were so many, but some remembered a pregnant lady. Rayne hurried over with the photo to show it to a woman who thought she recalled her.

"This is her." Rayne shoved the small photo at the woman who peered at it and nodded her head.

"Yes, that's her." Her hand went to her forehead thinking. "Yes, I remember her." She became excited. "She needed a shot of insulin. She was in rough shape, they wanted to admit her but she would not have it. She insisted she had to get home, but the doctor gave her a prescription and sent her to the pharmacy, over there." She pointed across the park to the small store.

"Thank you." Rayne reached for her hand. "Thank you so much!"

The woman smiled a small smile before walking away.

Rayne cried out, "Jace! I think we've found her." She waved her arms in the air to get his attention. "Over here, hurry!"

Jace and the man sprinted toward her. The man asked, gasping, "What's wrong?"

"Nothing, I think I've found Kelly." She turned toward the pharmacy and pointed, bouncing up and down excitedly. "Over there."

"How do you know?" Jace looked from her to the small building that was mostly still intact."

"That lady there," she said, pointing to the woman walking away. "She told me."

The long dark braid swayed as the woman moved, revealing a small tattoo on the back of her neck. The man in the vest's eyes lit up and he took off after her, spinning her around and instantly wrapping his burly arms around her.

Jace and Rayne, with Boon in tow, took off for the pharmacy to find Kelly. The man saw them and followed along with the woman. It was like a race with each of them bolting for the one place he was finally sure he would find her.

Jace burst through the door of the small store and stopped looking around at the crouched people staring at him wide eyed. Rayne came in with Boon right behind him and asked, out of breath, "Is she here?"

Jace stood silently gazing at the people, none of them were Kelly and his heart sank. "I don't see her." His eyes fell to the floor.

Rayne called out. "Kelly? Is there a Kelly in here?"

"Over here," a voice called out.

Jace's eyes widened, and he stood a little taller.

"We're over here," the voice shouted again. "Please, we need help."

Just then the man in the leather vest and woman came through the door and stood behind Jace and Rayne. The moment was surreal, no one moved trying to locate where the voice had come from.

Again, the voice called out, the words seemed as though they were shaking. "Please help us, she needs help."

"Where are you?" Jace cried.

"Behind the counter, please hurry."

The woman shoved past the others and ran for the counter with Jace right behind her. Kelly lay on the floor with blood seeping into her eye from a nasty gash on her forehead. The woman quickly ripped a pack of gauze from a package and began to work on the cut. Kelly cried out and gripped her abdomen, her face twisted in pain.

The woman placed her hand on Kelly's very pregnant belly and immediately drew it back. She looked up at Jace and the others. Fear written across her face told Jace something was wrong, and he dropped to his knees next to her.

"Kelly, I finally found you."

Kelly looked at him, her face twisted as the next contraction rolled over her. "I couldn't find you," she whispered, "I called you but it went straight to voicemail."

Jace's jaw clenched as anger rose up within him. He was on the mountain and the signal was sometimes spotty. He was angry with himself for not being there when she needed him. One last hoorah, he'd told himself when he and Ian headed for their favorite camp spot. One more party. His mind swirled with what could have been or he should have done and his gaze wandered away from her.

She squeezed his hand and grimaced. "I think the baby is coming." She squeezed his hand harder and growled.

Jace looked at the woman whose hand was on her tummy. She nodded yes to him. "Stay with her while I gather some things." She ran for supplies, snatching things from shelves and returning to her. Rayne appeared with some blankets and pillows, gently tucking one under Kelly's head.

Kelly eyed her suspiciously and then looked at Jace. "Friend of yours?"

Rayne covered her with a blanket. "He saved me after the first quake, I came to help him find you." She smiled sweetly at her, but she just looked away and back to Jace.

"Of course, he did." she sneered.

Her comment was almost accusatory. Rayne stood and took a step back, shocked. The woman helping her reached for Rayne's hand, shaking her head.

"I'm going to need you."

Another contraction hit Kelly and she sucked a long breath over her teeth then gasped out at Jace. "Always off doing something else."

"I'm sorry, I—" He gently swiped the hair from her face wiping the last bit of blood away. "You're hurt. I wanted to... I tried..."

He couldn't make a complete sentence and her eyes looked at him, condemning him. Rayne was becoming angry, after all he'd been through. The rage rose up her face like a whistle ready to blow.

The woman touched her arm. "Can you help me?"

Rayne looked at her and the anger began to subside. She nodded, "What can I do?"

The woman asked the man to get everyone onto the other side of the counter to let them be alone while the time grew close. He moved an old lady to a chair he'd grabbed from the waiting area at the pharmacy. A few others were gathering things people could need. Bottles of water, bandages, snacks, and pain relievers. All settling into a circle near the checkout.

The woman pulled Rayne aside. "I'm going to need help."

Rayne nodded at her but said nothing.

"My name is Amanda."

"Rayne." She held out her hand. "Who is he?"

"He's my brother, Ant."

The curious look on Rayne's face again made Amanda giggle. "His name is Anthony, but we always called him Ant."

Rayne looked at her and smiled. "I wondered; it seemed a bit odd. You know, he was looking for you when he stopped and helped us. He's kind of scary looking but was the only one to try and help us."

Amanda laughed, "Yeah he looks scary, but he's just a big teddy bear."

Just then Kelly cried out and Amanda looked at her watch. "Won't be long now." She pulled a box of Nitrile gloves from the shelf and reached for some rubbing alcohol and nodded to her brother. He checked on the little old woman before coming to see what Amanda wanted and Rayne tilted her head watching it with a slight smile.

"Whatcha need, Manda?"

"Well, I'm not sure, but we might need a little muscle."

Ant held his arm up and flexed. "I might be able to help with that."

Amanda sighed and pulled a few more items from the shelf nodding at them to follow her. Boon whimpered and shoved his nose up under Rayne's hand who unconsciously petted him.

When they came round the counter, Kelly's eyes were full of fury. She was berating Jace for everything. Amanda swung her head slightly side to side and pursed her lips. She instructed Anthony to remain at her head should she need to be held down or helped to sit up. Jace would hold her hand and provide support while Rayne would help by offering things Amanda needed. The contractions were less than a minute apart and Kelly screamed through each one.

She glared at Rayne and snarled. "You think you can just roll on up and keep him from his family? If he wasn't off saving some… some whore, he'd have been here."

Rayne's eyes filled with tears. Jace looked at her apologetically, while Ant shoved her shoulders down. Amanda's face gave away her emotion as one of disgust. She waved her gloved hand to her. "It's ok, I got this, why not see if you can be of assistance to the elderly couple."

"Take that mangy thing with you," Kelly snarled.

Rayne held Boon's collar, dropped her head and turned. "C'mon Boon."

"Rayne, I'm…" Jace looked to Kelly and back to Rayne.

Rayne smiled an uneasy smile. "I know." She turned and went around the counter to sit with the others.

EIGHTEEN

THEO

Theo, propped up on the sofa, took the broth Cami handed him before she sat near his feet. Joey took up a place cross legged on the floor up close to the coffee table and heartily began devouring his stew while Doug sat in his recliner.

Theo looked at the stew and protested. "Hey, how come he gets the good stuff and all I get is the juice?"

Cami glared at him, and he smirked at her. She stood and snatched the cup of broth and stomped off into the kitchen. Theo looked at Doug who sat smugly crossing his arms leaning back in his chair.

"What did I say?" Theo's hands outstretched, palms up in confusion.

Joey snorted and giggled while shoving another bite of stew in his mouth.

"You got something to say?" Doug scowled at him.

Joey's eyes shot to Theo and then to the kitchen. He wrapped his arms around himself and started making kissing motions. Cami walked back into the living room and spotted Joey pretending to make out with himself.

"What the hell are you doing?"

Joey's eyes opened and stared at her. His head dropped without a word, and he immediately went back to eating his stew. She shoved a bowl at Theo and sat down.

"Cami, I didn't mean to…"

"Oh, good grief, just eat your damn stew."

Theo looked at Doug, who shrugged his shoulders and changed the subject. "We need to talk about what is happening."

"Exactly what is happening?" Cami's look shifted to one of worry.

"Well," Doug began. "I don't exactly know but I heard from a ham radio operator up north who told me that there have been some small eruptions at Yellowstone."

Cami's eyes widened. "Yellowstone?"

"Yeah, but more than that, there have been earthquakes all over the place. Something is causing this."

"Like?"

"We don't know, but the one thing I do know is that if Yellowstone really goes, Denver will not be safe. The ash will be too much and will bury this city."

"You mean we have to leave here? Where will we go?"

Theo cleared his throat and Cami turned to look at him. "We need to try and contact Rayne again. To tell them. They can't come here if…" His voice trailed off and he looked back to Doug.

Doug nodded to Theo, picking up the thought. "This is why we are having this conversation. We wanted to get some input from you, and Joey as well."

"Me?" Joey perked up. "You want to know what I think?"

"Sure." Theo smiled in his direction.

Doug beamed, "Theo reminded me earlier of what smart ideas you have, Joey."

Joey sat up a little straighter and grinned into his bowl. Everyone munched on their stew in silence while they tried to process all that they'd just gone over. They had to figure out where they'd go, and some way to reach Rayne. Obviously, via phone, but there was no way to know if she would have a signal, so all that they could do was keep trying.

Suddenly Joey grinned, "Hey how about we go to Aunt Frida's down in Albuquerque?"

Theo's brows went up questioningly toward Doug, and he put his hand to his chin. Toying with his beard with his index finger and thumb he thought a moment before grimacing and shaking his head. "Two things," he began. "First it is hot as hell there and there is no water. What if we have to try and scrounge and can't find any? Second, wouldn't that send us west? With all that is happening out west, I am not sure it's such a great idea to head toward it."

Cami and Theo sat nodding, while Joey cast his eyes down because his father shot down his idea.

"Whatever we do, we need to decide before we try to contact Rayne again. We will have no way of knowing if we will get another chance… That is if we can even reach her at all." Cami's voice quivered. "What about Missouri? My friend Rose is there." She looked at her father expectantly. "You remember Dad, the one that went to DU with me and hated her roommates, so she stayed here, like, most of the time."

Doug nodded and looked to Theo. "What do you think?"

"Don't look at me, I barely know where I am, let alone what Missouri is like."

"I remember Rose," Joey exclaimed. "They have a super cool cave on their ranch."

"What if we try for Albuquerque? Rayne will have better luck finding us at Aunt Frida's. We can scrounge supplies and other things and give her a week to find us, but also, she won't have to travel all the way up here. If it is going to get bad, she will never make it here and won't know where we are. At least at Frida's we can leave her instructions and maybe supplies for the trip to Missouri." Cami's voice trailed off, "But maybe she'll make it to Albuquerque before we have to go?"

Theo nodded, looking first to her, then to Doug and Joey. Doug's lips pursed and Joey fist pumped in excitement that someone had liked his idea.

Doug thought with his hand on his chin. "I agree that it's an easier journey at the moment. Why not look at it in sections, first one Albuquerque, then another across into Oklahoma toward your Grampa's old farm and if we need to, further into Missouri. We can leave notes along the way if we have to move on."

Theo sat nodding in agreement. His mind was elsewhere, he was still unsure of why Cami was angry with him and felt like his place here was shaky at best. Suddenly uneasy, he offered a smile that never reached his eyes. He was grateful for all of their help.

Strange this situation. He's always been in charge. In charge of servants, companies, people. He'd never needed to ask anyone about what to do but generally gave the orders. He liked Doug who the kind of father he wished his own would have been. Cami adored him and Joey idolized him. Theo was envious of their family and looked down to his stew and quietly began to spoon some into his mouth.

"Good, isn't it?" Joey smiled with a mouthful of potato.

Theo nodded and continued to silently eat his stew. She was a complete mystery to him. He had no idea why she was mad and feared that if he said something she would get even angrier at him. His emotions were all over the place. He thoroughly enjoyed the challenges she offered but wasn't sure how to navigate them, either. He found her exhilarating and interesting.

While he was eating and thinking about what an interesting person she was, she returned to the room and slapped a magazine on the table. "I don't know where it came from, but someone knocked on the door and left this," she scoffed and walked away.

Theo picked up the magazine and thumbed through it noting the article about himself. He recalled this one, it was a rag that tried to make famous people look bad. There were a dozen photos of him with different women on his arm calling him a playboy. He sighed and tossed it onto the table.

When she returned with after dinner coffees for everyone, except Joey who got hot chocolate, and sat down she looked at him smugly and said, "Slumming these days are you?"

"What the hell Cami? Someone tosses an old rag magazine on the doorstep and I'm suddenly some kind of dog?"

She looked down and then to her dad for support, but he shrugged and went to stirring his coffee. He slyly winked at Theo and grinned.

"I didn't ask to be stuck like this you know, and now you're mad at me for a two-year-old magazine?"

Theo scoffed and tried to get up and go back to the room but faltered as he tried, and Cami slid up under his arm.

"Oh, good grief," she mussed. "Don't go getting all worked up. Let's get you to bed."

Joey snickered and she raised an eyebrow at him, narrowing her eyes in a veiled threat for his outburst.

She helped him into the bed and allowed him to sit up while she arranged the pillows, cursing and mumbling under her breath. "I swear guys just run at danger, never thinking about the outcome." Her voice raised and she scolded him. "Why you punched Rob out is beyond me. You had to know he would look for revenge."

Her words made no sense to Theo, he was just trying to protect her. He reached for her arm as she continued to grumble and arrange the pillows behind him. "Honestly, all you playboy types are the…"

He leaned into her and kissed her. Stunned, she just sat on the chair beside the bed and said, "Why did you do that?"

"Because I've wanted to since you snuck out of the break room."

"What?" She smirked, "I think you were thinking of Blythe from the looks of the magazine article."

He reached for her hand and held it a moment before speaking. "No, Miss Camilla James, I wanted to know more about the girl who refused to throw herself at me. I am not what they portray in that magazine." He paused, "Well, yes, I was. I used to be that guy, but no one wants to spend time with brainless airheads who spend more time in the bathroom getting ready for all the parties than they do at the actual party."

She looked at him suspiciously, "Seriously?"

"Yeah, Cami. Seriously. Please don't think of me that way, it's not who I am."

"Oh, good grief," she huffed and stood. "Get some sleep."

"No Cami, we need to call your sister. Can you get your dad and my phone if I'm not allowed to get up?"

Her face changed to worry about Rayne, and she nodded, turning to leave. He held onto her hand a moment longer and brought it to his lips, kissing it before releasing it.

NINETEEN

RAYNE

"It was fast for a first baby." Amanda's eyebrows went up when she looked at Jace and then emerged from behind the counter wiping her hands with a paper towel. "Mother and child are doing well." She grinned and looked at Jace. "Her gestational diabetes should begin to resolve but we need to keep an eye on her blood sugar for a while."

Rayne's heart sank thinking about the way that Kelly treated him. Berating him and putting him down. It made her angry and she sulked in the corner with the dog. She was glad the baby was alright but completely disgusted with his baby mama. She sat mindlessly petting his head and whispered to him, "She didn't like you any more than she did me."

A husky voice spoke up from the other side of a display, "I've known people like that. Don't take it to heart, they don't like anyone. It's not you."

Rayne looked at him, eyeing his bulging arms and black vest, curious about the biker guy with a heart. "Ant, is it?" She eyed him and smiled. "Thank you for everything."

His face blushed a little, and he shuffled his feet, but didn't speak. Amanda walked up beside him and put her hand on his shoulder. "He ain't much for words." She smiled at him. "But he is always there in a pinch." She punched his arm and giggled. "Right, big bro?"

He wound his arm around her shoulder. "I was so afraid for you when the first explosion hit." He pulled her closer, dragging his knuckles across the top of her head.

"Knock it off, Ant, or I'll tell the little lady here all kinds of shit about you."

He eyed her and smirked. "I'm gonna have a look around outside, I'll be right back."

Amanda pulled up a section of carpet beside Rayne and plopped down laughing, "He really is just a big ole' teddy bear."

"Well, he definitely looks like a bear." She chuckled beside her. "How's the little family?"

"Them?" she said, thumbing over her shoulder, "Yeah, that? I don't even want to comment on her. She's a real piece of work, that one. I get it that she was scared and all alone, but he was recounting what had happened, how their friends died and he couldn't help them and was so afraid for her. All she could do was accuse him of sleeping with you."

"Me?" Her eyebrows shot up. "I don't understand at all. All I did was help him find her."

"It's the type, honey. In all likelihood she got knocked up just to trap him. Happens all the time, never works out."

Amanda shook her head and ripped open a Power Bar offering one to Rayne. She smiled at her, reached out and took it gratefully.

Rayne laughed, "I tried to get Boon to eat a piece, but he snorted at it and slumped down onto his front paws."

Ant returned with some Gatorade and handed one to each of them and produced a stick of jerky for Boon. Ripping it open, he offered it and Boon's tongue lolled, salivating for the meat stick.

He let him have it and scratched his ears absently while looking through the window. "It looks pretty clear out there, most of the chaos at the hospital has subsided to just the fire. The whole building is burning now."

Rayne looked up at him, his blue eyes a stark difference to his dark hair that hung in front of his eyes. She liked him and Amanda both. Kelly on the other hand? Jace had explained how she got pregnant, and he felt a responsibility for the baby but damn, she was a piece of work. Rayne feared that Jace would leave her; alone in this big city was not her idea of fun. Boon was not on the nice list either. She hugged the dog, "Don't you worry, buddy, I won't leave you."

The rumbling began again, low beneath them. Suddenly, with a loud crash the whole store began to crumble. Ant ran for the old woman and shooed the others out of the store while Amanda, Boon, and Rayne made for Jace and his family. When they rounded the corner Jace was covering his son with his body as the ceiling tile fell on him. Kelly was screaming for him to take care of her, with little concern for her child. Amanda and Rayne each crawled under one of her arms and hoisted her to her feet. Rayne screamed over her shoulder, "Boon, get Jace." The dog seemed to know what she wanted and gripped his sleeve softly, pulling on him and whining.

"C'mon Jace!" She cried, "We gotta get out of the store."

He looked up and turned, cradling the small bundle, and ran for the door emerging mere moments before the roof caved in. Jace fell to his knees as Rayne and Amanda dropped Kelly onto the grass before turning back to check on Jace. Ant ran over to check on him and the baby as well. Kelly climbed to her knees, screaming that someone needed to help her, almost jealous of the attention given the infant.

The old woman walked up to her and slapped her across her face. "Shut the hell up already."

Amanda snorted and almost laughed out loud and Jace grew panicked. He didn't know what to do. Rayne reached out for his arm and assured him everything would be alright. She leaned in to see the baby and cooed at the small human. "Awww Jace, he's perfect."

Kelly stomped up and smacked Rayne's hand away from the child and jerked the baby away from Jace. Amanda rushed in to support his tiny neck, instructing her on the care of a newborn. Kelly raged at her to get away. "It's my baby and I will take care of it how I want." She plopped the child down on the grass and glared at Jace, who was still standing next to Rayne. "Well? Aren't you going to get the kid a bottle or something?"

"A bottle?" Amanda asked. "In this mess? Where the hell are we supposed to find a bottle?"

She sneered at Amanda, "I didn't ask you, did I?"

Jace hurried to the rubble of the pharmacy and Ant joined him in search of bottle fixings. Amanda and Rayne stood next to each other watching as she did nothing for the baby that was crying on the lawn less than an hour old.

Rayne scoffed, "No wonder he wanted out."

Amanda looked at her in shock and Rayne rolled her eyes. "He told me that he wanted to break up with her once he saw what she was like, but she'd gotten pregnant, presumably from what he says, on purpose, and he wouldn't abandon his child."

Amanda stood nodding knowingly. "That never wins them what they think it does and more often than not actually pushes the guy that was on the fence about leaving off that fence and into a run. Any woman who would do that just to trap him ain't no kind of woman those guys want around."

"I know many who were trapped in such a way and stayed to be forever miserable hating their partner." Rayne looked down, she completely understood that.

"Well, maybe Jace will see the real her and make a better choice for himself and his son. Things are not all about the mom and custody these days. I'm going to make notes of all this for him." Amanda sneered toward Kelly, "She's no mother and never will be if she can't even hold the baby."

Rayne sighed, "Well I hope she snaps out of it for the baby's sake and comes round."

Amanda nodded and shook her head looking toward the store where Ant and Jace emerged with armloads of supplies. "For their sake."

Rayne changed the subject. "I talked to my sister in Denver, and they said that they're having quakes, too. I'll be going there, and I thought it would be with Jace and Kelly and the baby, but those plans seem to be out the window."

"Denver?" Amanda turned to Rayne shocked. "Quakes in Denver?"

"Yeah, and a volcano. They said Yellowstone was rumbling and a dormant volcano in Denver erupted."

"Shit," Amanda hissed. "I talked to a friend in Montana a few weeks ago who told me they were having cluster quakes surrounding Yellowstone. Ant and I were planning to go east just before this one started."

"My sister seemed to think there was more going on

than just some quakes."

They sat silent for a few moments before the same sound came from her pocket, Bwee Boop. Her voicemail notification, they must have gotten a signal. Amanda quickly looked at her phone and dialed a number while Rayne listened to her voicemail.

Her eyes widened and mouth dropped open at the words she heard. When the message was over her hand fell to her lap, she had no words at what her father's voice had told her. Tears burst from her eyes and rolled down her face, but words still escaped her.

Amanda saw the streaks in the dirt on her face and moved to her. "Rayne, what's wrong?"

"That was my dad. He's had news from others in other parts of the world. This is not local, and they are leaving Denver, headed for Albuquerque." Tears ran down her face. "What does this mean?"

"I don't know, but if you still have a signal, you could try calling them, and from here Albuquerque is easier to reach than Denver." Amanda placed a reassuring hand on her shoulder.

"I'll try." She pressed the call button and put it on speaker and they both listened as the phone rang. It went to voicemail.

"You have reached Theodore Brandywine; please leave a detailed message and phone number and I'll return your call later."

"Hi this is Rayne, I wanted to talk to Cami. I hope this is the right number." She looked at Amanda who leaned in on the phone and spoke. "Message received for…" She glanced at Rayne who spoke. "For Albuquerque but don't know the exact address of Aunt Frida. Call me back if you can."

Ant and Jace had returned with ready to drink formula, bottles, powdered formula, thermometer, receiving blankets, hats, booties, you name it they grabbed it, cleaning out the baby section of diapers, onesies and even some toys. Neither of them realized he wouldn't be into toys for a little while. Rayne and Amanda laughed to each other at the silly guys fussing over the baby. A moment of happiness and joy in an otherwise screwed up world.

"Do you think Jace will still come with me and bring his family?"

Amanda wrinkled her nose, "I don't know. That one is a piece of work. She feels threatened by any woman."

"Isn't that like the post-partum thing?"

"Perhaps, I'll get Ant to work on it. They aren't going to be safe here alone."

"What about you and Ant? What will you do?"

"I don't know that either," she snorted. "We need to get out of here, but don't really have any family. It's been just him and me for years."

"Why don't you come with us?" Rayne asked excitedly, smiling at her.

"Would it be ok with your family?"

"Of course, they already said to bring Jace and his family. I'm sure they'd love you."

Jace and Anthony went back into the store for more supplies and Rayne looked around at the people that had escaped the store. The older couple sat together chatting. She figured them to be in their late sixties or seventies, a woman about forty or so, and two guys, young surfer types. One blonde, the other dark, sat on either side of Kelly animatedly chatting with her about her bravery and beauty. She was sucking it all up and Rayne scoffed.

Amanda went over to her, and saw her holding the baby, head down and shoving a bottle of cold formula at him growing agitated because he wouldn't take it. She asked to see him. At first, she jerked the child back, but Amanda told her he needed to be checked over and that she should take care of herself for a while. "I really need you to check your blood sugar again." The only way she got the child was to encourage her to take care of herself first.

Rayne admired Amanda's prowess in the art of what she'd always referred to as 'schmoozing'; telling Kelly how important self-care was in this time and that she should let her take on the burden for a little while. After all that she'd been through, she was entitled to a moment's peace.

The baby was wailing, and Kelly looked at him like he was annoying her. She handed him over along with the bottle and said, "I do deserve a little bit of me time, don't I?"

Both of the young men nodded at her

enthusiastically.

Rayne was just about to gag over her selfishness but was grateful that Amanda managed to get the baby away from her so that they could care for him properly.

The bottle was full of the formula and was not sterilized or even rinsed out before she poured it in. They knew there was no way to sterilize it but at least could wash it with bottled water. Amanda held the infant while Rayne rinsed a much smaller bottle and scrubbed it vigorously with the bottle brush before dumping the water and giving it a little bit more to rinse it a second time. They'd placed some formula into a baggie that Amanda had tucked beneath her armpit to warm it up.

It was still a little cold, so Rayne asked Anthony to come over and put it under his arm. He protested until Amanda gave him a look.

"Come on, Manda, do I have to?"

"Do it, Ant," she growled and he tucked the pouch of milk under his arm.

In about ten minutes it was warmed up to body temperature and Rayne poured it into the small bottle. There were about four ounces and Amanda knew the tiny infant wouldn't take it all. She hoped for at least two ounces.

He hungrily latched onto the small nipple and quieted immediately. Kelly sneered at the two women caring for the child, with Jace leaning over Amanda's shoulder and Anthony looking on.

"Hey, I need something to drink too," she shouted at Jace and the others. "We don't want my sugar to go haywire. Do we?"

The blonde-haired man raced for the pile of stuff the guys had brought out and grabbed her some snacks and a soda, bringing it back to her and they continued to listen to her go on about being a model and coming to L.A. for an acting career.

The others were just grateful that she was entertained so that they could take care of the baby.

TWENTY

CAMI

They'd made the call and left a voicemail for Rayne, hoping she got it and would understand where to go before turning in for the night. Something still bothered Cami about the magazine. She couldn't figure out where it came from. Who had knocked and left the thing on the stoop was a complete mystery. It bothered her. Who knew Theo was at her house besides Rob Stearns? He'd given her a ride home one day when Blythe went home sick, but it was suddenly terrifying that he still remembered where she lived.

She tossed and turned all night until finally climbing out of bed to go check on things. She found Theo sitting up in the living room watching out the front window and asked him, "Coffee?"

She'd startled him and he spun his chair around, his wide eyes meeting hers. His finger was against his lips and he waved to her to get down. She fell to the floor and crawled over to his position on her hands and knees. He wrapped his free arm around her while his other hand held the gun pointed through a tiny sliver in the curtains.

He peered out into the darkness at the figure whose hands cupped his face as he tried to look into the house. Cami looked up and followed his finger toward the figure and slouched her lips against his ear.

"Who is it?"

"I think it's that guy from the office. Does he know where you live?"

"He drove me home once."

Theo put his hand up and pointed to the doorknob. It moved, slightly jiggling, and then stopping. They peered out the window and he'd moved off. Theo moved toward the back window and told Cami to get down behind the sofa.

Theo stood at the edge of the curtain peering out into the yard and waved to Cami that he could see him and to get down.

Silence in the room made her breathing sound like roaring in her ears as she waited for Theo to return. Now she was sure that it was him who had left the magazine. It took forever before Theo came back telling her he'd left.

"He got in his car and pulled off down the block, I doubt he will stay gone but the sun is almost up so we probably won't be bothered except by magazine drops for the day. If he is going to do something he will wait for nightfall."

Theo helped her up and smiled when she tripped and fell into his arms. She stood, trying to right herself and seem cool and collected when she was anything but. Rob scared her and it frightened her to think he was working alongside her all this time.

"How 'bout that coffee?" Theo asked.

She shook it all off and headed for the kitchen to put a pot of coffee on. Her dad would be up soon anyway and would want some as well.

The coffee perked and she got out creamer and sugar and put it all on the dining room table along with mugs for her, Theo, and her dad. Once the pot was done she brought the hot dark liquid over and pulled up a chair next to Theo.

"Do you think he will come back?"

"Likely, he didn't like being put down like that."

"He scares me. With what he said about me back at the jeep and what they did to you; I don't even want to think about what he has in mind." She shuddered and poured the coffee.

"I have to tell you Cami." Theo looked at her sternly. "If he tried, I'd kill him."

Cami nodded, knowing she wouldn't care if he did. She was not the girly-girl type but not entirely a tomboy either. The thought of it bothered her but Rob was evil, and she was fast finding her terror unsettling.

Doug came strolling into the room rubbing his eyes, "Did I smell coffee brewing?"

"Your cup is right there dad," Cami said and began to pour the coffee into his mug.

"What are you two doing up so early?"

"I was keeping watch and Cami just got up a little bit ago herself."

"Dad, someone was creeping around the house."

Doug's eyes opened wide, and he hurried to the windows to look outside. "Who was it? Did they leave?"

"Yeah, they're gone, but I think it was that Rob guy that we ran into earlier." Theo took a long drink from his cup before continuing while Doug continued to look out the window.

"He drove off up the street that way," Theo thumbed over his shoulder. "I'd bet he will be back tonight. This guy is a menace, and I really don't want to have to kill anyone."

Doug looked over at him, eyes wide. "Do you think it would come to that?"

"I don't know but after what he said he wanted to do to Cami, I'd have no problem doing so if he went anywhere near her."

Doug smirked and returned to the table to refill his cup. "Honey, could you whip up another pot? I think we're gonna need it."

Cami got up and took the pot to the kitchen and

Doug whispered to Theo, "Do you think this guy would hurt her?"

"Worse," Theo scowled.

Cami returned to the table with her own fresh cup and asked what they were talking about.

"I think we need to leave here today." Theo seemed agitated.

"You may be right," Doug agreed.

"We could take the Jeep, but I don't think everything will fit in it."

Cami smiled at Theo. "We have a small enclosed trailer out back that dad uses when we go camping to carry supplies. Some things are still in it."

"Oh, that would be great, I think we need to pack plenty of water. Cami and I also grabbed some water filters and other needs from the camping store that we should take."

"Good thinking," Doug said and rose, moving toward the desk on the wall. He pulled open the drawer and grabbed a pad and some pens. "Perhaps we can make some lists this morning and start packing up to leave by what? Noon perhaps?"

Theo's head bobbed up and down, his hand grasping his chin in thought. "I think we could do noon. We should wake Joey, that boy thinks of things we never would."

Doug nodded to Cami who hopped up and hurried

for Joey's room, returning moments later with the groggy boy who was complaining that the sun wasn't even up yet.

"Hey Joe, we were hoping you could give us some more of your good ideas," Theo said, winking at Doug and Cami.

"Oh?" Joey yawned rubbing his eyes.

"Yeah, we are going to head out for Albuquerque this afternoon and thought you might like to help us plan," Doug added.

Joey's eyes widened and he hopped up onto his knees in his chair. "We are leaving today?"

"Yeah, we think it's best," Cami sighed.

"Ok, what can I do?"

Doug handed him a piece of paper and a pen and said, "We are making lists of what to bring. Cami will write all the kitchen and food stuff on hers; Theo will write all the camping stuff and what clothes and linen to bring, I will write tools and such, and you… how about you help think of and write down anything else we might need?"

Joey eagerly grabbed the pen and paper. They began by noting the obvious things, food, water and some cooking utensils that Cami scribbled on her pad. Theo added water purification to his list and Joey recommended the oven shelf could hang somewhere and not take up much space.

"Why the oven rack?" Cami asked.

"Well, what if we gotta cook over a fire? We could

put it on the rocks to hold the pans up."

Doug patted him on the back and Theo fist bumped him. "Great idea, we should definitely add it."

Cami rose to go cook breakfast but took her pad with her, if they called out something for her list she added it. This continued through breakfast and then each of them headed off with their lists to find the things they'd decided they needed. Everything was piled in the living room in order of what was considered most necessary to luxury. Cami insisted her shampoo and conditioner was a necessity while Joey insisted on the game case that held backgammon, cards, dice and other games. It looked like a briefcase and was small in comparison to other things.

"What about a coffee pot?" Cami called from the kitchen. "We have the one we've run on the inverter, but I don't know how well it will work."

Theo called out, "I grabbed a camping one from the store. It's in the boxes we brought back that day in the garage."

"Oh yeah," Doug mused and hurried for the garage. "Give me a hand will ya?" He waved to Joey.

"I'll help." Theo jumped up.

"It's ok, we've got it. You're still in rough shape, don't push too hard. I'm gonna need you sharp riding shotgun. We don't know if that character will come back."

"What character?" Joey asked.

"Nothing," Doug said and shoved him out the door to the garage.

TWENTY-ONE

JACE

Jace hurried from one task to another while they sat in a small circle on the lawn of the hospital. Amanda and Rayne watched with looks of disgust at Kelly. She'd been complaining for the past hour while the others tried to decide what to do. Anthony spoke to Jace telling him that he and Amanda had decided to go to Albuquerque with Rayne. Jace looked at the three of them longingly but knew Kelly would never go for it.

She sat entertaining the surfer boys while Jace brought her snacks and food. She never asked to see her son again once Amanda had fed and changed him. She and Rayne made a small cradle out of the wagon Rayne had pilfered from the small thrift store.

He looked at the two women and then back to Kelly wondering if that was what his own father's choice was. He felt lost and confused, needing to be a good father but decidedly against what he thought he'd do with that ring in the small box. There was no way he was going to marry that woman.

Another quake rocked the area and more parts of the hospital caved in. The older man and woman bade them all farewell and decided to return to their house. Amanda tried to get the couple to go along with them, but they insisted they'd just be a burden and would be fine in their own home. "It's where we want to be." The old man looked at her sympathetically and grasped her hand. "We'll be fine."

The other woman, the one in her forties would go with them, her name was Maria, and she had no family in L.A., her family lived in France, which she felt she had little chance of reaching.

The two young guys wanted to head for the beach to see what was happening there and Kelly wanted to go. She felt sure she could be discovered in the chaos when the news agencies caught sight of her in all of this and began digging through her purse for her makeup.

Jace didn't want to go to L.A. He wanted to find a safe place for the baby. She whined, but sat and pouted when he finally stuck up for himself and the baby and said no. The very thought of bringing the baby into that mess angered Jace. She kept trying to convince him that they needed to go, and he flatly refused. He joined the small group chatting about Albuquerque and cooed at his son in the wagon.

Kelly decided she was going to the beach and jerked

the handle of the wagon, nearly tipping the baby out of it.

Boon growled at her and she dropped the handle. "That thing wants to attack the baby," she screeched.

Rayne glared at her and then at Jace who was arguing with her about it. Amanda had picked up and soothed the infant while Kelly stood screaming how she deserved to be discovered.

"Fine, then go," Jace growled at her. "But my son isn't going."

"You can't do that."

The two guys moved in behind her as though they planned to fight with Jace. Ant rose to his feet and stood behind Jace.

"I'm leaving here," Jace yelled. "You need to come with us."

"And if I don't?"

"You'll never see us again."

The two guys whispered in her ear and smirked at Jace. She stood defiantly with her arms folded. "I'll call the cops on you and tell them you kidnapped my baby."

"The hell you will," Rayne exploded. She'd had enough too and walked up and punched her right in the nose.

Blood exploded from her nostrils, and she screamed, backing away. "My face! Oh, my face."

"I'll give you some more if you don't quit. You need to come with us and get your baby to safety, he needs his mother, even if she is a piece of shit," Rayne growled at her.

"Jace Walker, you never were good at anything. We're through," she scoffed.

Jace almost looked relieved but tried to get her to come with them anyway. "Kelly, think of the baby. We need to take care of him."

"You weren't even good in bed," she sneered, "I should have left long ago to find a real man." When Rayne balled up her fist and drew it back again, and she screamed, "Keep the damn thing, I'm outta here."

"Thing?" Jace went after her. "You called my son a thing?"

"IF, that is… if it's your son," she called back and rounded a corner.

"Oh, good grief," Rayne sighed.

"No shit," Amanda scowled. "Good riddance, I say."

Jace stood looking down at the grass but said nothing. Ant flung his arm around his shoulder. "Tough break my man."

"It's been getting worse and worse with her. I tried to break up, but then she told me she was pregnant. How can she not care about the baby?"

Amanda crooned to the baby and approached Jace. "Not all women have the mothering instinct. Some people are just too selfish to care for other human beings... Even their own children."

She handed him his son. "He's better off."

Rayne didn't want to interrupt but cleared her throat. "I'm sorry, Jace." Her head hung, "It's just... Well, it's just that I couldn't take it anymore. If she knew what you went through to find her." She growled and looked at him harshly and turned away.

"We need to get going," Amanda said.

She took the baby from Jace and instructed him to go with Anthony to find a vehicle.

Jace looked at the ladies and eyed the bunch before snorting, "Aren't we a bunch?"

Anthony failed to see what he thought was so funny, shrugged and walked over toward the car lot on the corner. They looked at the cars and Jace recalled the struggle in the streets to get where they were, wondering if something more versatile might be a better option.

"Hey, Ant," Jace said.

"Yeah?"

"Getting here a lot of the streets were blocked. I am not sure how far we will get in a vehicle."

Anthony gripped his chin and looked around at the debris on the road. "Hummm." His eyes turned to Jace. "Can you ride a bike?"

"You mean a motorcycle?"

"Yeah."

"Sure, I rode dirt bikes all my life, not much different."

"Manda rides, not sure if the other two do but I can take one and either you or Amanda can ride the other."

"What about the baby?"

"I grabbed one of those baby backpacks from the pharmacy. I know it is not ideal but I'm sure Manda can figure it out. Let's go to the motorcycle dealership over there and see what we can find," he said, pointing to the large motorsports place across the road.

"I get it but, Boon. There is no way he'll ride on a motorcycle and I'm not leaving him."

"Well, we will look for a sidecar or trailer or something." Anthony put his hand on his shoulder, "We'll figure it out."

They went inside and it was deserted, which Ant said was fortuitous and Jace looked at him curiously. He laughed, "Manda makes me play those word of the day games with her. She tells me just cause I'm a biker, don't mean I gotta be illiterate."

"Are you?"

"Illiterate? No," he scoffed. "I have an MBA. I work for one of the smaller studios in L.A."

Jace tilted his head quizzically and Anthony laughed, "Long story my friend, it'll make for a nice campfire tale."

They hunted around the dealership and found Softails for Amanda and Jace, he wasn't comfortable with the bigger bikes and a Street Glide for Ant. Anthony nodded approvingly and motioned Jace toward the door. "Let's go get the girls. We can hang out here for a bit while we set the bikes up and figure out how to transport Boon. We'll need to add some bags to each of them to carry our gear."

They hurried to the girls; they didn't want them left out in the open too long. When they got there Kelly and the two guys were back and trying to take the baby. Kelly stood back while the blonde one smacked Amanda who refused to let go of the child.

Rayne and Maria struggled with the other man while Kelly laughed maniacally behind them.

"What the hell?" Jace growled.

Ant was already running toward them. He plowed into the blonde guy who'd hit his sister, knocking him to the ground. Jace grabbed Kelly by the arm, dragging her forward while he distracted the dark-haired guy poking him in the head. When he turned his head, Rayne reached out with a right to the jaw knocking him to the ground.

He got up glaring at Jace who released Kelly to tackle the guy. Kelly turned to run but Maria grabbed her by the hair dragging her to the ground. She struggled to fight, still sore from giving birth only hours before and gave up easily.

"Wait." Kelly poured on the fake tears. "I forgot my insulin and when I got here and saw him, I was sad. I only wanted to be with my baby."

Rayne reached out and gripped her hair, nodding to Maria and sneered at her. She leaned down and whispered to her through gritted teeth, "Two things are gonna happen here today and neither of them end with you taking that child. I'll kill you myself if you try. You got me?"

Kelly nodded; her eyes wide. She hadn't heard Rayne get angry before. Even with all the mean things she said to her.

Rayne continued, "First, you are going to reassure Jace that he is the father of that child."

"But I don't know if he is," she sobbed.

"Irrelevant, you will say you were trying to make him mad. Second, you will decide once and for all if you are coming with us or staying. Jace and the baby are coming with me and the others."

"Ok… Ok," she sobbed.

Rayne climbed off of her and hoisted her to her feet. Jace and Anthony held the other two. The blonde was already sporting a growing shiner from Anthony while the dark-haired guy was nursing the bloody nose Rayne had given him.

Anthony whistled when he saw Rayne, "Damn, Ray, you got a decent right hook."

She nodded and heaved Kelly's arm, shoving her up next to the others, making her stagger into the center of them where she tried to straighten her clothes and wipe the dirt off of herself.

Anthony scolded the two guys, "You hit one of these ladies again and I'll break both your arms and leave you for dead." The two nodded, fear in their eyes.

Anthony was not a small man. He was big and imposing, downright frightening at that moment. They gathered the supplies and the ladies and brought everyone to the dealership. Kelly and the two boys, as Ant had taken to referring to them because they acted like children, sat on the benches; she scowled and glared at Amanda, who refused to put the baby down at this point, as well as Rayne. Giving them accusatory stares and mumbling under her breath.

The two guys sat on either side of her, the blonde saying, "I'm not sticking around for this shit. That big dude is scary as fuck."

The dark-haired guy agreed, "We don't need to go nowhere. I'm headed for Rodeo Drive, there is some shit worth millions there. We can just take the best house in Beverly Hills and live like kings."

It piqued Kelly's interest and she nodded whispering to them, "I just want the baby."

"What for?" the blonde asked.

"He's my son, you asshole," she sneered at him.

Rayne overheard this and knew she didn't want him because of her motherly instinct but because she wanted to hurt Jace for choosing them over her.

Jace wanted her to come along, to be a mother to his son. They all knew what was happening across the country from the phone call and that it was not safe here. The risk of tsunami, and even bigger quakes increased with every moment they stayed.

Kelly reluctantly agreed to go with them and would ride on the bike with Jace. Amanda could carry the baby and Rayne would ride with Anthony. Boon would be in the sidecar they found alongside Jace's bike. Maria and the two guys could ride their own and would carry a pack on the rear of the bikes. Each rider's bike would be equipped to carry a backpack and all bikes would have saddlebags as well as other smaller ones made for the handlebars and tanks.

They'd spend the night in the dealership preparing the motorcycles for the trip. Jace and Anthony lined up the bikes and began to attach the gear while Maria gathered backpacks and other items like chaps, jackets and helmets for each person.

Rayne and Amanda prepared some food out of the things they'd taken from the pharmacy. Tuna with crackers, some pickles and chips were set out. Kelly asked for the baby, but Amanda refused without Jace right beside her. "Oh, honey, he's sleeping so peacefully. I honestly think you need to take some time to care for yourself. Have you checked your sugar?"

Once he sat with her, she was allowed to hold the

baby. Rayne and Amanda watched, disgusted at how she tried to use the child to get to Jace but he didn't care. He just wanted to be a family and was willing to brush off what she'd done, asking Amanda if it could have been hormonal.

Amanda reluctantly agreed things could get better once the chaos was less. She didn't believe it, she'd seen this kind of narcissistic behavior before and knew it was all an act but wanted Jace to feel better. It was after all quite the whirlwind day, with the hospital blowing up, finding his girlfriend having the baby, escaping the store and having the girlfriend flip out like that had to have been hard on him. Kelly had just given birth. Even though it was fast and easy it still takes a toll on a woman and her hormones could be messing with her.

Jace overheard Amanda whispering to Rayne, "Kelly has had children before."

Rayne's eyes widened. "Really? How do you know?"

"The episiotomy scar, from what I saw delivering the baby, she's had at least two before this one. You want to know what else?"

"What?" Rayne whispered.

"At one point she may have had gestational diabetes, but she hasn't had a single blood sugar test outside normal that I've done. I think it resolved like most do early on and she was using it as an attention thing."

Jace's gaze fell to the floor when the girls looked his way. He didn't want to admit it but somehow, he knew she was right. Kelly held the baby haphazardly and finally gave him to Jace so that he could change his diaper. Amanda had already warmed a bottle for him and offered it to Jace so that they could feed him together, but Jace shook his head.

"Can you do it?"

"But, don't you want to?"

"Yes, but I need to keep an eye on her. She is up to something, I'm sure of it and I don't trust her or them. I want the baby as far away from her as possible right now."

Amanda took the infant and agreed to care for him. She, Rayne, and Maria went into one of the sales offices with the child and settled in for the night while Anthony stood guard over the door and Jace kept an eye out at the entrance. Anthony convinced him that he needed to grab some shut eye and pulled a sofa in front of the door to the office for him to sleep on. Ant said he would wake him in a few hours to switch out the watch and he settled down on the sofa and tried to sleep.

Twenty-Two

Theo

The supplies were organized, the trailer, backed into the garage alongside the Jeep, was loaded and ready to go, complete with extra gas cans. Empty ones, but they were sure they'd be able to find gas in abandoned cars. Joey said they needed the awl so that they could just punch holes in stranded cars' tanks, another of his good ideas.

But it was far past noon when they finally felt ready and had loaded the trailer and Jeep. In spite of the fact that they knew Rob would return they decided it was safer to start out in the morning instead of trying to navigate the city at night. All they needed to do was to pull the Jeep out and connect the trailer to it and they would be ready to go.

Theo was sure this was a bad idea but went with what they wanted to do. He insisted that they take turns keeping watch. Doug and Joey would take first watch while he and Cami slept on the sofas.

Doug had one of the guns at the front window while Theo kept the other one with him. Around midnight Doug woke him for his watch and Joey, determined to be helpful, remained at the back window.

Theo noticed that he was nodding off and rose to wake Cami when a loud crashing sound echoed from one of the bedroom windows, waking Doug and Cami.

Theo knelt beside the sofas with his finger over his lips for silence, nudging Cami to the floor. Sounds came from the front door as well and he whispered, "There's more than one."

Doug waved them toward the hall to the garage. Joey and Cami went out into the garage while Theo stood at the entry to the hallway with Doug. "We need to wait until they are all inside," Doug whispered to him. "Do you think you can keep them occupied and make noise while doing it so that I can pull the Jeep out and hitch the trailer?"

Theo nodded and Cami's voice from behind whispered, "I'll help."

Doug handed her the gun and they waited quietly in the dark hallway. Doug would wait to hear the noise inside before opening the roll up door. Joey stood by the door ready to open it at his father's signal. There was no sense defending the house when they were planning to leave anyway, Theo just hoped that they could escape without anyone getting hurt.

Theo could feel Cami's hand shaking as she aimed the gun into the darkness and whispered to her, "Relax, we are only giving them time to get ready and a diversion. We have one inside from the bedroom, another over by the living room window. I'm just waiting for the guy at the door to finally break in then we'll let 'em have it."

"Are we gonna kill them?"

"Probably not, we're just gonna fire into the room to make noise and pin them down so your dad can get the Jeep ready."

She gasped, bringing her hand to her mouth to stifle the sound when the front door burst open and someone crept into the darkness.

They could hear Rob barking out orders, "Find them and bring me that bitch."

"It doesn't look like anyone is here," another voice said.

"Check the bedrooms, they're here."

"Now!" Theo whispered and fired a shot into the darkness.

Cami followed with one of her own and someone cried out they'd been shot. Cami made a low whine of fear and Theo put his hand on her shoulder. "Give me the gun, go help your dad. I'll keep them pinned down.

Cami hurried down the hallway to help her dad and Joey get ready. Joey stood at the door once she arrived to let Theo know when they were ready.

He could see shadows moving in the darkness and fired again, first from one gun then the other.

Rob cursed and called out, "Where are they shooting from?"

The guy who'd been shot just moaned and wailed and Theo searched the room for the third man. His position was dark without any light from the outside, but the living room had a dim light coming in from the curtains they'd moved from the windows.

Theo prayed they'd be ready soon because once the light grew stronger, they'd be able to see him. To the left a movement caught his eye just before the man lunged at him. He turned to shoot but the bullet went wide, shattering the back window.

He grappled with the man on the floor and fired again when he was able to get control of his hand. The body went limp on top of him, and he rolled him off hopping to his feet but remaining in a crouched position.

Joey whispered from the doorway, "Ready."

"Ok, go get in, I will be right there."

His mind raced, hopefully they hadn't been smart enough to post someone outside. That was two down, but Rob was still in the room somewhere. His eyes strained to see anything in the dimly lit room. A gray light danced with the fine dust of the ash in the air.

There. He caught sight of him around the corner to the kitchen. For only a moment his head popped out and peered into the large open space. He called out for his friends in a whisper, "Randy? Did you find them?" His question returned with silence as Theo waited for him to emerge again. "Randy?"

His head popped out and Theo took aim on the wall he hid behind and he fired again, three shots through the wall. The loud moan was unmistakable, he'd hit his mark. He turned and ran for the garage door, bursting through and hopping into the passenger's side of the Jeep.

"Go… Go… Go!" he shouted, and Doug pressed the gas pedal careening out of the driveway.

"Is everyone ok?" Theo reached back for Cami's hand. It still shook, tears rolled down her cheeks leaving streaks in the gray dust that covered her face.

Ash was really beginning to fall but the filter on the snorkel to the Jeep's air intake was a good one. He recalled the story Cami told him about how Doug loved to go off roading back in the day and that was why the jeep was raised with a snorkel. It felt kind of sad that lately he hadn't done much more than tinker with the vehicle adding new upgrades. He didn't really know the man, but his lips pursed in almost admiration at the difference between Doug and his own father. Doug working on the Jeep for the day when Joey could take it and have some fun, when his own father would never even let him do such things, calling it an embarrassing sport.

They each put on the dust masks they'd grabbed from the home repair store to keep from breathing it, but they had to stop a couple times to clean the filter for the Jeep before they made it to Pueblo. Getting out of the Denver area took pretty much all day. The highways were a mess with cars and collapsed overpasses. They headed west to reach the 470 loop in hopes it would be less congested and passable. They were able to go a couple of long stretches before having to exit to get around a collapsed overpass. By the time they reached I-25 everyone was exhausted. Joey fell asleep around the time they hit the southbound highway after being awake all night and Doug insisted on driving even though Cami offered a few times.

It was slow going but they found a little motel about ten miles from the city where the owner was still trying to operate. Theo still had cash and grabbed two adjoining rooms. They were grateful to stop for a respite. Although they could have made it to Pueblo and even past it, they needed to rest. They were all on edge for hours, the adrenaline from the early morning exit and the constant watch for threats along the way in the murky gray landscape was taxing and their senses and reaction time were slowing.

"We need to rest," Theo said. "We have no idea what we might hit in Pueblo and don't want to navigate a city at night."

"You're right," Doug conceded. "How are we going to do this?"

"I thought Cami and Joey could share one room and you and I the other." Theo waved to the adjoining door. "We can keep it open. This room has a small kitchen with what looks like a propane stove. We could cook some food and hunker down."

"Sounds good but let's put Joey with you on watch and stagger them. Cami is still upset about firing the gun and Joey hasn't had any training yet. They can have them but at least there will be one of us with gun experience on watch at all times."

"Good idea," Theo nodded rubbing Joey's head with his knuckles. "Looks like it's you and me." They headed over to the kitchen to have a look around.

"Theo, you need to try and grab a nap, you've been up," Doug said.

"Nahh, I'm good. Since Joey and I are on watch together, you and Cami can hit the hay in the other room while we dig out some food and supplies. I can clean the filters again. This way we can eat after you get some rest and grab some shut eye while you and Cami take watch."

"Why don't you and Joey take the first watch? Then you could sleep."

"You wanna cook?"

"Nooooo," Joey whined. "Dad's cooking is awful. Can't Cam cook, dad?"

Theo looked at Cami who seemed annoyed, "What's up?"

"Is this a girl thing? I'm the girl so I get to cook?" Her hands flew to her hips in defiance.

"I'll cook," Theo grinned. "I am the master of pbj's and potato chips."

"Yum," Joey licked his lips and rubbed his belly.

Cami scoffed and stomped toward the kitchen. "I should let them eat sandwiches," she grumbled. "Dad, you and Joey get some shut eye for now, it'll be about an hour or so to get things ready."

Theo moved up behind her whispering in her ear, "You have to admit, your cooking is pretty amazing. That beef stew was mouthwatering."

She turned, staring only inches from his face as he smiled at her. Shoving past him she scowled, "Help me dig out some food for dinner and we might as well grab coffee while we're at it. Check to see if we have water."

Theo turned on the faucet and water, clear and clean flowed from it. "We need to grab the jugs and fill them up. This must be a spring or perhaps a water tower, it has good pressure and is clear."

Doug and Joey closed the curtains in the other room and shut the door to get some sleep while Cami and Theo tended to their own tasks. Theo smiled at her over his shoulder each time she passed by him. She looked at him side eyed, but he knew she was coming around.

Twenty-Three

Rayne

At some point in the night Kelly decided to curl up next to Jace who slept with his son against him and tried snuggling in. Amanda had fed him less than an hour ago and placed him with Jace. She was on watch with Ant and mentioned how she saw her slither over to him about thirty minutes after. In his sleep he put his arm over her and continued to snore.

Amanda looked at Anthony and whispered, "I don't trust her."

"Neither do I," Rayne whispered from behind them and tip-toed over to sit with them on the other side of the showroom where she'd been silently watching. "She's up to something, I can feel it."

"Why do you suppose Jace puts up with all of that?" Amanda asked.

"For the baby," Rayne sighed. "He said some stuff in the few days it took us to find her. I think his biggest thing is some kind of daddy complex."

"What?"

"His mom blamed him for his father leaving. Not that he was ever hers, no man leaves his wife for the side chick," she scoffed. "But anyway, she told Jace all his life that he was worthless and I think he believes it. The funny thing is? He's super smart. Did you know he got into MIT?"

"Really?"

"Yeah, but funding kept him from going. He just wants to be the dad he never had and prove to his mother that he is not a loser."

Anthony stood and dragged his hands through his shoulder length hair. "I gotta hit the head ladies, you got this?"

"Sure," Rayne whispered.

Amanda's eyes fell to the floor, and she sighed, "You like him, don't you?"

"Who?"

"Jace."

"Oh," she laughed, "Sure, but not like that. I respect what he's trying to do. He saved my life, I owed it to him to help him." She glanced over to where Jace, Kelly and the baby slept. "I can't believe she acted like she did toward me. I'm no threat to her."

Amanda's eyes raised and moved toward where Jace was sleeping peacefully. "He does have that kind of sad boy appeal, doesn't he?"

Rayne snickered, "You like him."

Amanda shook her head, "Oh," she stuttered, "It's just, um…"

"I think Ant is pretty hot actually, what's his story?"

Relieved not to have to go into the whole Jace issue she smiled at Rayne. "Really?"

"It's funny because he works for a pretty big company in some kind of executive job. He keeps his tattoos covered at work but afterward he likes the biker lifestyle," she laughed. "He isn't part of any club, kind of a loner, but goes to the bars where the bikers hang out and he's friends with many of them. He could never join up because of his job and kept the two separate."

Her words trailed off as Anthony emerged from the bathroom. She whispered, "He's like two completely different people. Watch how he approaches things, you'll see."

The girls snickered as he approached but he looked alarmed. "Where's the two dudes and Kelly?"

"They were right over…" Amanda paused and stood. "Ant, they were literally right there not two minutes ago. Rayne and I walked to the back window to check the back but never left the room. We circled the room and then came back here in less than a minute." Her voice rose and she screamed, "The baby! Where's the baby?"

Everyone was awake at this point; groggy murmurs filled the space. Jace got up panicked, turning in circles, his eyes scanning the room for Kelly and the infant. "The baby." He threw his head up looking at the ceiling. "She took the baby!"

He dropped to his knees with his head in his hands gripping his hair. The room watched as he screamed, got up and flung the chairs across the room. "I'll kill her myself," he cursed.

Rayne's eyes widened; she'd never seen him so angry. Even when those guys in the park tried to stop them, he didn't lash out like this.

Jace's anger grew, and he slumped onto a chair, pulling on his hair as he growled. "I don't even know where to look."

Rayne tried to console him, but he didn't want to talk to anyone and turned away after glaring at her. She felt powerless and walked throughout the building looking for any clues.

Amanda came up to her whispering, "What are we gonna do?"

"I don't know," she paused and looked at her, "We have to find the baby, there is no way Jace will leave without him."

Amanda's head hung. "I feel so bad, I feel like it's my fault. I was on watch."

"Don't feel like that. I was with you. We never left the room; I can't even figure out how they did it. Like seriously we barely took our eyes off of them all."

"Let's think back," Amanda said. "Everyone was in the same place when Ant went to the bathroom."

"Yeah, I remember eyeing the whole room, checking everyone."

"Ok, when is the next time you can recall looking over the room? I remember looking over when we were talking about Jace and seeing Kelly under his arm."

"Me too," she said, eyes closed. She gasped and opened her eyes, "The dark-haired guy... He wasn't in his spot."

"Are you sure?"

"Yeah, think Amanda," Rayne pleaded. "Do you remember the guys sleeping when we made the rounds?"

"Come to think of it, I was too focused on Kelly to register it but they were both gone. I didn't think anything of it because Maria had moved out of the office to the line of chairs. I figured they'd moved too. I remember seeing her come out and lay across them. I just assumed she didn't want to be alone."

"When was the last time you saw Kelly?"

"She was still there then, but I do remember her cuddling the baby and thought briefly that perhaps it was just stress that caused her to act the way she was. Shit, I remember this specifically." She looked up, her eyes darting in all directions searching for the memory or anything that would help her recall.

"My guess is that she was awake the whole time and working at pulling the baby in and away from Jace," Rayne growled. "That sneaky…"

Anthony walked over putting his hand on Amanda's shoulder. "We found where they left from, the door is still propped open and there are cigarette butts by the door. I think they'd been planning it all night."

"I think so too," Rayne said. "We were just trying to go over what we recalled about the movements and positions of the others around the time you went to the bathroom. That's when we can't recall seeing either one of those guys. We were so focused on Kelly that we completely missed seeing them sneak out, one by one."

"They were quiet," Amanda said. "Almost as if they'd taken off their shoes or something. This was planned from minute one, I'm sure of it."

"How do we find them though?" Anthony turned to look at Jace who was growling to himself. "If we don't get a plan and fast, he is gonna be ready and head out on his own. I won't let him do that; we have to help."

"SHIT!" Rayne called out loud enough that everyone looked at her. "Where's Boon?"

Jace leaped up from his seat and called out "Boon, c'mon boy." He stopped and tipped his head up listening and then whistled.

A muffled whimper could be heard from outside. He ran out the door calling him, "Boon, where are you?"

Rayne's heart raced in fear for the dog and called out behind him, "C'mon Boon, where are ya boy?"

Outside the whimper and barking got louder but they couldn't locate it. Anthony put his hand up for everyone to be quiet, nodding at Jace to call him again.

Rayne craned her neck to listen in the silent air, hoping for a sign or sound of the dog.

Jace called him with a whistle, "Boon!"

To the left a yelping bark of the excited dog turned them all as one. They ran toward the end of the building near the street, stopped to listen and called again. The bark was louder, and Rayne could hear the scratches of Boon against the window of a car.

She gasped when she saw the frantic dog digging at the side of the door. "He's locked inside."

They raced to the car and Jace pounded on the window. Anthony pulled him back and produced a pen. Quizzically, we all looked wondering what he'd do with it. He held it like he would a knife and went to the passenger side window. "Keep Boon on your side."

Rayne and Jace tapped on the window cooing at the dog and trying to keep his attention off of Anthony.

He stabbed at the window with the back side of the

pen and it shattered. Reaching in, he punched the unlock button and Jace jerked the other door open for the dog, who pounced on him licking his face.

Rayne and Anthony looked inside the car from either side. Anthony found a couple of beef jerky wrappers and gripped them in his hand looking up at her. "That was how they lured the dog into the car so quietly."

He emerged from the far side of the vehicle carrying the wrappers and held them up for the rest. "They planned this," his voice angry as he crumpled them in his fist. "They knew the dog would sound the alarm and lured him into the car first." He growled, with an angry and agitated edge to his voice. "Those mother…"

Amanda stepped up beside him. "Anthony, where are you going?"

"To find them," he growled.

"But we don't know where they went. How are we supposed to find them?"

Rayne ran over to him and grasped his arm, he looked down at her angry but his look softened. "I think I know where they went," she said softly.

"What? How?" Jace ran up and spun her around.

"It just hit me; I overheard a conversation earlier. The guys wanted to go looting on Rodeo Drive and take over a house in Beverly Hills. That's gotta be where they went."

"Gather everything and get ready, they're on foot or

at least they were." Anthony looked at them, "Looks like it's L.A. first. We need to be careful because the only ones left in town are those who will look to us for help and we can't help anyone who can't help themselves," he paused, "and then there's the others."

"The others?" Rayne asked.

"The ones who stayed behind to loot and bring mayhem, they could be a problem. We need to make a pit stop first."

"What for?" Jace cried out, in a hurry to go find them.

"Protection," Anthony growled.

Amanda's expression changed. "Ant, do you really think it will be an issue?"

"Manda, if these guys took the baby and Kelly and their goal is to steal, who else do you think is out there still? Let's go," Anthony turned and headed back inside. "We need to get the bikes ready and head out."

In only moments everyone was on their bikes and ready to go. Rayne rode with Anthony and grinned back at Amanda when she wrapped her arms around his waist. Amanda gave her a thumbs up. Jace looked quizzically at the two women while he soothed Boon in the sidecar. Amanda and Maria were in the middle on their own bikes.

The roar of the motorcycles echoed off the empty city as they pulled out and made their way toward L.A. The pit stop was to be a small gun shop where Anthony knew the owner and in only ten minutes, they pulled up outside and parked.

He instructed them to wait outside and keep an eye on the bikes. "Be alert, we don't know who is left in the city, but I am sure whoever won't be that friendly."

He was inside for a good ten minutes, and Rayne was nervous. She could see that Jace was becoming antsy.

"What is taking so long?" he murmured. "It's been forever, and why can't we go in too?"

Amanda walked up to him with a soothing voice trying to calm him. "Trust Ant, he knows many people, some good…" she glanced inside the store, "And some not so good. He can get the kind of help we need to get your son back. We've helped one another and now we are… tribe, trust that." She put up her index and middle finger in a peace sign and winked at him.

His look was sullen, but he nodded at her and gave her the peace sign in return.

Rayne smiled at him and nodded, while Maria put her hand on his shoulder.

Maria hadn't said much but nodded to him. "You and that baby have been polarizing for us all, giving us a reason to want to be better in all of this. To rise up and not just be victims. We're all in this together and will do what it takes to get him back."

Jace looked around, his eyes reflected amazement at the support of practical strangers. Rayne had only been with him for a few days but knew Amanda was right. They were a tribe.

Jace's shoulders dropped, and he nodded to them. "Thank you," he said humbly.

"I don't know about you all, but I'm kind of looking forward to beating that bitch's ass right about now," Rayne smirked and winked at him.

Amanda and Maria smirked at her but Boon began to growl, the fur on the back of his neck raised, teeth bared as he glared across the street. Something was wrong. Rayne caressed his fur and glanced at Jace to see if he had his collar.

Amanda peeked inside the store and yelled out to Anthony, "We've got company!"

TWENTY-FOUR

CAMI

The sun dipped behind the mountain range leaving an orange hue on the gray skies. It looked ominous and foreboding. Cami looked at Theo, glad that he'd come along with them. She marveled at his comments of how he found her interesting and wondered if he still would have, even if the world wasn't ending. Recalling how he'd followed her out into the office she found herself wondering if maybe, just maybe, it would have been her instead of Blythe for once. Not daring to chase this train of thought, and suddenly feeling guilty for her jealousy of Blythe, she moved to place the food on the small table for everyone to eat.

They'd made dinner and woke Doug and Joey for food and then to have them take the watch.

Joey yawned emerging from the darkened room. "Mmm something smells good."

He hugged Cami and thanked her for cooking the meal before settling in at the small table.

"Dad," Cami said, handing him a plate. "You and Joey take the first watch. Theo is exhausted and so am I. We can keep them short but I don't think I could keep my eyes open."

"I agree, that'll work sweetheart," Doug said, kissing her on the head then clamping a hand on Theo's shoulder as he passed him to sit in the small chair in the corner.

While they ate, they looked at the map to check the route and find a better way around Pueblo. After the things they saw in Denver, and the smaller city of Colorado Springs, they thought it best they avoid Pueblo all together but there was really no way around it, they'd have to brave it and hope for the best.

Once they'd eaten, Theo went with Joey into the other room. Joey sat at the window facing the back of the motel while Doug sat in front looking out the one facing their Jeep and trailer of supplies. He was worried about leaving them out in the open and watched them like a hawk.

Hours passed uneventfully and soon it was time to wake Cami and Theo for their watch. Just as they were climbing out of bed and searching for coffee a sound by the door startled them. Theo stood with his finger to his lips as he peered silently out from the side of the blind. Doug tried to peek through the small peephole in the door, but it was blocked.

They knew this was bad and made sure to stand on either side of the door when Theo called out. "Is someone there?"

A voice from the other side called out, "You need to pay for the room."

"We paid for the rooms. As a matter of fact we paid double."

"Cash is no good anymore. We're gonna need what you got in that trailer."

"The hell you are," Doug called out.

"It's best if you cooperate so we don't have to call in some backup."

Theo peered through the side of the blind and Cami looked from the other window while Joey checked the back. Joey shook his head, he saw no one and Cami put her index finger up she could see only the one guy the same as Theo. He nodded for Doug to open the door. Cami remained at the window while Theo moved to the door's edge, ready with gun pointed at the opening while Doug opened the door slightly peering out in the darkness.

With the door open not even six inches Doug peeked out and handed the man the receipt for the room. "The room was paid in full, in advance."

"Well, money's no good anymore," the man sneered.

"It was when we rented the rooms," Doug argued. More to check for others and stall the man than anything else.

They didn't see anyone else until Doug opened the door wider and could see a woman and two small children standing behind the corner of the main office entry. The man lunged inside reaching for Doug and Theo grabbed him, flinging him to the floor and holding the gun in his face.

Doug glanced at the woman whose hand went to her mouth and touched Theo's arm to relax him. "Help him up."

Theo looked at him surprised and Cami questioned why her father had relaxed. She came forward with the gun uneasily positioned in her hand, finger still on the trigger. Her dad reached for it and she handed it to him. "Never have your finger on the trigger until you are ready to shoot," he admonished her.

The man now sat in the chair looking hungrily at the food covered on the table. "Call your family in here," Doug said in a gruff tone.

"No mister, they didn't do anything. It's just that it's been days, and we never went to the store and now they are empty. We would eat at the restaurant but the food there was taken by the owners when they left early yesterday morning."

"Call your family or else," Doug scowled.

The man's voice cracked but he did as he was told, "Gretchen, come in here." He looked up at them pleading as Cami and the others looked on.

"Dad I…" Her father's hand went up and she paused.

The woman and two children appeared at the door and Doug motioned them to sit before scolding the man. "You could've been killed." He pointed to the woman and children. "Then where would they be?"

The man's eyes filled, and fear shook him. "You have to think," Doug barked and turned away from the man.

"Watch them," Doug growled and went out to the trailer.

When he returned, he had an armload of food. He laid it on the counter and looked at Cami. "We may as well start breakfast since there will be no sleeping."

The children looked at the food with wide eyes and Doug's face softened as he waved the man over to his family and turned back to Cami. "Breakfast will be for seven, can I help you?"

Cami smiled and kissed her dad's cheek. "I got this, you go and talk to the man."

Doug sat on the second bed while the man and his family were lined up on the edge of the one closest to the door. He looked at the two young boys and asked, "Are you hungry?"

The youngest boy nodded his head while the oldest hid further behind his mother's arm. The woman regarded him suspiciously while the man looked confused.

"We won't hurt you," Doug said reassuringly. "But we don't want you to hurt us either." He glared at the man.

"We won't try to hurt you," the man said, hanging his head. "I saw you get food from the trailer and just wanted some for my family. I heard on the CB radio in my office that the volcano has started to erupt."

"What volcano?" Theo stepped up asking.

"Yellowstone, I think," the man sighed and looked up at him.

"We can't be here." Theo hopped up and began to pack. "We need to leave now."

Doug looked at him, his eyebrows meeting in the middle of his forehead and told the family to wait there, food would be up shortly. He followed Theo to the kitchen area where Cami was cooking and asked what the issue was.

Theo's hand brushed Cami's and he looked at her nodding. "Please hurry." Then turned to Doug, "I've seen models of what would happen if the caldera ever went and this whole area will be under feet of ash. We need to get moving."

"What about the family?" Doug whispered.

"If they stay, they will die," Theo said, matter of factly.

"How do you know all this?"

"My father's company has done some drilling up near there and they did a study on how likely it was to blow and what would happen if it did. That project is part of the reason I decided to leave his company and come to Denver." He looked around the room and noticed the kids eating hungrily. "They need to come with us."

His agitation was enough to bother Cami and she asked him, "Is it really that bad?"

"It could be," he sighed, and sat down to his own plate alongside her. "We just need to go, and soon. There does not seem to be a good way around Pueblo, and we don't know when the eruption started or how big it will be."

"Let's move over next to Dad and Joey and talk to the family."

They grabbed their plates and moved over to talk with Doug and the family. He'd already figured out that their family lived in Mexico and that he and his wife had never met them. They weren't sure where in Mexico but were willing to leave their small motel if they had to.

Theo explained about the ash and that he was concerned for them. Doug encouraged them to go with them at least to Albuquerque.

The man looked suspicious and asked, "Why would you help us when I tried to take your things?"

"Because we're not so different," Doug looked down, then back to the man. "I'm not sure that I would not do the same for the sake of my children. Do you have a vehicle?"

"I have my truck," the man said.

"When you're finished eating, go pack and then pull it around the front. We'll pack up and be ready to go in... let's say fifteen minutes?"

The man nodded and headed for the door leaving his wife and children to finish eating. "I'll be back in a few minutes with the truck, then Gretchen can help me with the kids' things," he said, and turned to go out the door.

"Hey," Theo called after him. "What's your name?"

"Mario," he called back.

Theo looked at the boys and smiled at them. "And you are?"

Neither answered and he looked up at Gretchen, his eyebrows up. She nodded and pointed to the older boy. "This is Alejandro and that is Marcus." Her arm wrapped around the younger boy.

"Pleased to meet you." Cami walked over and reached for Gretchen's hand. "I'm Camillia, Cami for short." She pointed to the others. "That's Doug, my dad and over there is Joey, my brother. This is Theo." She put her hand on his shoulder.

"Is that your husband?"

Cami laughed, "No, he's uh... A friend?" She looked at Theo who smiled at her and winked.

Cami collected the dishes and started to wash and dry them, replacing each into the cabinets where she found them while Theo and the others began to gather their things. Gretchen went to their place to gather clothes and other things while Mario filled water jugs, gallons and anything else that would hold liquid. Joey and the boys helped load them into the back of his truck.

Gretchen placed suitcases and whatever they had left of food outside their door and Mario loaded it with the help of Doug. When she was finally done, she appeared in the doorway with a crate holding a fuzzy gray tabby cat.

Mario objected, "We can't take the cat Bebe'."

Cami scooted over to poke her fingers through the holes, "We can't leave it. It'll die."

Gretchen and the children objected and begged, finally Mario gave in and told them to get into the truck. Joey was already in the Jeep with Doug in the driver's seat. Cami climbed in and Theo waved for them to follow as he climbed in riding shotgun. The small group pulled out and onto I-25 southbound headed for Pueblo.

TWENTY-FIVE

JACE

A man emerged from the alley with two others behind him. "Well, lookey what we have here," he sneered and took a step toward the ladies. "Gentlemen, I think we have found ourselves a group of ladies who need protecting and will do anything we like in gratitude." Boon growled and bared his teeth. The fur stood on his back as he pulled on the leash to escape Jace's grasp.

Jace had half a notion to let go of the dog but only feared they'd hurt him. "Leave us alone," he shouted.

"Looks like this guy needs a lesson, too." He turned to wink at the women then glared at Jace. "Kill him and the dog."

The women were prepared to fight and stood beside Jace. Rayne reached down and petted Boon's head, cooing at him not to worry. She stood with her putter in hand, ready to swing while Maria had a knife and Amanda had picked up a couple of bricks. Jace had fire in his eyes; he was done with being pushed around and would not fail. He was sick of this world already and would find his son. His mother's words haunted him, "You're never going to amount to anything but a loser Jason."

The anger was boiling up, ready to explode when Anthony came out of the store, handing him a shotgun. Jace's eyes narrowed on the three men who'd planned to kill him, and he raised the weapon and pulled the trigger. He missed the men completely and didn't intend to actually harm them, but he wanted to. He wanted to kill them, he wanted to kill Kelly and the two idiots she took off with.

The men retreated, cursing, back into the alley they'd emerged from calling back threats. Jace's hand frozen on the gun, he stood rigid, his eyes piercing the still dark alley.

The sun had come up but only slightly and there were many dark areas for the worst of men to hide. Jace shook with anger and determination, he would not miss another.

Anthony was followed by four men also carrying guns. At first their appearance behind Anthony made Jace step back until he realized they knew Ant.

The men stood with guns aimed at where the three had retreated, looking at Jace, impressed with his willingness to just shoot.

"Damn dude that was badass," one joked, while Anthony tried to settle Jace down.

"He's seen a lot already," Anthony explained.

Jace sat on the edge of the sidewalk absently running his hand down Boon's back, the soft fur warm and sleek. He murmured to the dog, "I won't let anyone harm you my friend." Boon looked up at him, his tongue lolling, enjoying the attention. He licked a big sloppy kiss up Jace's cheek that brought him out of his moment.

He stood and thanked Anthony and his friends. "I don't know what they would have done."

"Well, I have a pretty good idea of what they wanted to do," Amanda shuddered.

Jace and Anthony both glared at the alley, their eyebrows tightly pinched together. "If they come back, they'll be meeting their maker," Anthony growled.

Rayne's phone made a beep indicating a low battery and she held it up, finding she had two bars. She quickly hit redial and tried to reach Cami. After three rings a male voice answered.

"Hello?"

"Hello," she nearly shouted. "Hello, this is Rayne. Is Cami there?"

She put the phone on speaker so that everyone could hear. The service was spotty and broken up but the familiar voice of her sister's excited voice came through.

"Rayne? Rayne, is that you?"

"Cami," she sighed, tears rolling down her face. "It's so good to hear your voice."

"Hi, honey," her dad's voice boomed through the phone.

"Daddy!"

"Yes, honey, it's me. You have to listen."

"But, Dad," she cried.

"Rayne! Listen to me, we may not have a signal for long."

"Ok," she sniffed.

"We left Denver and are on our way to your aunt Frida's house in Albuquerque. Do you remember Aunt Frida?"

"A little."

"I'm sending the address in a text right now. The ash has started falling from Yellowstone and it won't be long before everything is covered. Please honey, get there as fast as you can. If we aren't there, look in the knothole in the old tree out in back of the house for directions."

The phone began to crackle, and the signal broke up. She held it in the air, turning to try and find the signal again.

"Dad… Dad, you're breaking up."

"Love you, hon.. Ease get to Aun… Don't waste ti…"

The call dropped and she punched the redial button over and over, but the signal was lost. Tears fell freely from her eyes, and she crumpled onto the curb holding the phone, turning it over in her hands.

Jace sat beside her and asked to see it, he wanted to get the address off of it in case anything happened, or it died. He quickly jotted down the address and shoved the small paper in his pocket before putting an arm around her shoulders. "Don't worry, thanks to you, we know where to look for them and once we get my boy we will go straight for Albuquerque and your family."

She smiled up at him and nodded, wiping her face.

One of the guys that had come out of the store cleared his throat, "Did anyone miss the whole Yellowstone volcano part of that conversation?"

"Yeah, that kind of threw me. How do they know that?"

"My dad has some friends on the ham radios that hear things all over the world." She stood and walked toward the group. "They were already getting ash from Dotsero. He said there is more going on. It's not just Yellowstone, earthquakes and volcanoes were going off all over the world the last time we spoke. He mentioned something about tectonics but I have no clue what that means."

Jace did. He knew what it meant. "It means that the company I was going to work for was right. The crust is unstable and the floating plates that sit atop the molten core are shifting. We could be looking at years of winter and ash filled skies." He looked at Rayne, "Your dad is right, we need to hurry up and go east."

Anthony told his friends to get their people and meet up with them on Rodeo Drive; that they would continue on in search of the baby. He hugged his friends and thanked them for the protection and bade them hurry. They may need help once they found them and instructed them to bring the bikes because of the possibility of impassable roads.

Jace and the others set out after Kelly and the baby. They weaved through the streets and debris with relative ease and stopped when they reached the beginning of all the ritzy stores. Jace knew Kelly would go for the clothes and shoes and turned his bike toward a specialty store with shattered windows and a sequined dress hanging out torn on a long shard of glass. A small trickle of blood streaked a jagged edge of the window next to the dress, but no one was inside. They moved from store to store along the road, all looted with shattered windows.

Jace's hopes began to fall as they neared the end of the road and Anthony approached him. "It don't mean nothing, they could have been and gone. According to what Rayne overheard they planned to head for Beverly Hills and so will we. We will find him." He slapped his shoulder and moved off.

Jace looked down at a pile of clothes and shoes by the door of the shop he was in front of. He reached in and pulled up a pair of dirty leggings. He held them up calling out to the others, "Hey, aren't these the pants Kelly was wearing?"

Amanda raced over and grasped the pair of filthy pants. She observed the crotch area and noted some soiled areas. "This was her alright. I'd also bet they are looking for some feminine products as well from the looks of these."

Jace continued to dig through the pile of discarded clothes and items finding the swaddling blanket that the baby had been wrapped in. Worry for the child overwhelmed him and his face twisted into a mask of despair as he held it close.

"Right," Rayne said. "We're on the right track. Let's check the convenience store across the intersection and the pharmacy. My money is on the pharmacy for what she needed but they may have wanted some beer and supplies from the other one. Let's split up. Jace, you go with Amanda and Maria to check the convenience store and we will go to the pharmacy. Meet back here in a few minutes."

When they returned to the bikes, Anthony and Rayne had baby bottles, formula, diapers, a few varied kinds of medicines and a case of water. Jace and the others had snacks, and chips, a whole bag of beef jerky and another with nuts and granola bars in it. They had armloads of Gatorade as well as candy.

"We didn't find any sign of them. The beer cases have been completely emptied though; they could have been here but we just don't know." Boon sniffed lustfully at the bag of jerky until Jace offered him a piece, warding him off until later.

Anthony held up a bag full of pills and first aid items. "Most of the narcotics are gone but there were plenty of antibiotics and other medications. We grabbed a bunch of Advil and Tylenol. But, I found these seriously good masks."

"What do we need those for," Maria's eyebrows came together curiously.

"Ash," Anthony said. "If we start running into the ash this is gonna be something we will need. There were also some bottles of oxygen. We will have to be careful but if we do run into some ash we will want to totally close off the baby and he will need to breathe."

"Good thinking," Amanda said, glancing around. "I'd like to check the pharmacy one more time before we go."

"Why?" Anthony asked.

"Nurses see things we need that others might not notice. You guys get everything loaded somehow and I'll be right back."

"You can't go alone," Jace hurried to walk alongside her.

"Ok."

While they packed the items away and strapped the case of water to the back of Maria's bike, Jace and Amanda headed back to the pharmacy. It was only about five minutes before a loud crash echoed down the street. Amanda and Jace emerged from the pharmacy with bags in hand. They stopped and stared up the road at three people running around a corner about four blocks up.

"Jace, c'mon, I think that was them."

They ran to the bikes and hopped on slinging the bags onto the handlebars. "Let's go, now!"

The roar of the motorcycles starting up bounced off the buildings and made it seem louder than it was as they closed in on the trio.

The bikes circled the three and Kelly stopped turning and faced them holding the child over her head as though she would drop him.

Amanda gasped, her hand to her mouth in fear and terror rocked Jace to the core.

"Kelly, what are you doing?" Jace called out to her.

"Get away from me," her shrill voice screamed.

A large man appeared behind them, reached over her head and lifted the child from her hands. She spun round on him, scratching at his arm screaming, "Give me my baby."

Rayne walked up to her and spun her back around winding up and letting her fist fly right into her face.

She spun and fell to the ground sobbing, "My baby, my baby."

Jace was beyond rage at the moment the way she'd threatened the child. He gripped her hair and lifted her head staring into her face, blood running from her nose down the front of her new sequined shirt. "Gather your shit." He threw her to the ground.

The two guys shook in the grips of the men they'd met at the gun store begging. "Listen man, it was her idea," the blonde said.

The dark-haired guy nodded. "She made us do it."

Jace waved them off and the guys released them. The two of them scrambled away cursing at the group while Kelly sobbed on her knees begging Jace.

He walked away with his son. "Pick her up, we need to get on the road."

Twenty-Six

Theo

"I feel better giving her the address instead of having her guess. She's only been there a handful of times," Doug sighed.

"Me too dad. Don't worry, they'll be on their way in no time, and we will see her again."

"Daaaad I really gotta go."

"Why didn't you go before we left," he sighed as they pulled off into a rest area to take a bathroom break. "I'd like to chat with our friends behind us and check on things before we try to roll through Pueblo."

"I didn't have to go then." Joey smiled and danced in the seat.

"Make it quick," Doug told Joey and turned to Cami, "I'm going to tell them what we know about California."

Joey hopped out of the Jeep running for the building to use the bathroom. Just as he did, the other two children made a dash for the restroom as well.

"Sounds good, I can drive if you want," Cami volunteered.

They met at the back of the trailer with Gretchen and Mario. Doug smiled at them warmly while Theo eyed them, he wasn't entirely convinced of their trustworthiness.

"We spoke to my daughter in California, and it seems as though they too are having some problems," Doug offered. "This thing seems to be widespread from what I've heard."

"How did you speak to her? Our phones aren't working." Mario eyed them.

"Oh," Doug laughed. "Theo has a satellite phone and occasionally there is a signal in her area."

"We've tried and tried to call our relatives in Mexico but we can't get any signal," Gretchen whined.

"Would you like to try my phone?" Theo asked.

"Could we?"

"Sure, I'll go get it." Theo turned and went to the Jeep for his phone. Something deep inside him said don't trust them and he couldn't figure out what it was that caused him to feel like that, but his senses were hyper aware and looking all around.

He returned and placed his thumb on the screen while holding it up to his face and it beeped. He then punched in an eleven-digit code to unlock the phone, handing it to her to dial.

"You will need the country code if you are calling out of the United States."

She nodded and began to punch in the numbers. Holding it up to her ear she listened. The phone went straight to voicemail, and she hung up. "It's not working." Tears welled up in her eyes.

"Try again," Theo urged. "This time leave a message. We can't always reach anyone but leave a message for them. If they get a signal, the voicemail will come through and they will know you all are ok."

She looked at the phone and it was locked. "I need the code, the phone locked."

Theo reached for the phone. "Here, let me see."

She held it firmly, "I can do it."

"Actually, no, you can't." He stood with his hand out, curious as to why she wanted to do it herself. "It is biometrically programmed for me. But, I will unlock it so you can call again."

She reluctantly handed him the phone and he unlocked it. She held it in her hand looking at him a moment too long and it locked again.

"It's locked." She looked at it quizzically.

"Yeah, sorry. I should have let you know you need to dial in ten seconds, or it locks." He took the phone and unlocked it again, handing it back to her. She dialed, waited for the voicemail and left a message that said that they were fine and moving south toward the Mexico border on I-25.

That struck even Doug as curious, and he looked at Theo questioningly. He slightly nodded not to discuss it at the moment. He raised his eyebrows expectantly. "Feel better?"

She tipped her head and looked at her husband. "Wha?"

"That you let your family know you're ok." he smiled. "Doesn't it set your mind at ease a little bit?"

"Oh, yeah," Mario laughed. "It sure does."

Joey and the boys were taking a long time in the bathrooms, too long in fact. Doug shot Theo a look and a nod and said, "I think I better go before we leave as well."

Mario instantly got uneasy and said, "Hey, I'll go with you."

Theo wanted Doug to be able to check on Joey alone just in case and said, "I gotta go, too, but don't want to leave the women all alone. Let's take a minute to grab some snacks for the road out of the Jeep for your boys." He reached behind and shoved the phone into his back pocket and thumbed the handle of the gun in his belt. Something just felt wrong even though he couldn't place what it was.

They grabbed some snacks and Doug returned with the boys. "They were writing on the bathroom walls," he laughed. "And you don't want to know what they were writing."

Cami giggled and Gretchen looked horrified. "Boys will be boys," Cami shook her head and cuffed Joey in the head while walking toward the Jeep.

"Do you ladies need to use the restroom?" Theo asked. "Doug, can you escort them? Mario and I can use the side of the vehicles while they are gone."

Cami laughed again, "After all, the world is a man's urinal."

Gretchen looked at her strangely and followed her. "What does that mean?"

She laughed as they approached the restroom, "It means, men will pee anywhere."

The girls entered the bathroom and immediately screamed. Theo ran for them just as Doug pulled open the door. They entered together to see why. Two women lay naked and dead inside on the floor. Theo grabbed Cami by the shoulders while Doug grabbed Gretchen and shoved them out the door. They all ran for the vehicles shouting for Mario and the boys to get in.

"Go." Doug shoved Gretchen toward her truck, "We need to go, right now."

As they were climbing into the vehicle bullets whizzed over their heads. The vehicles tossed dust and ash into the air as the tires spun and fishtailed, pulling out of the rest area.

Five minutes down the road no one dared speak as they watched behind to see if anyone was following them. Once they were sure they were in the clear, Theo let out a loud sigh.

"I knew something was wrong; I just felt it." He glanced back at the road again. "I thought it was Mario and Gretchen, but I guess it was just something else."

"No, I agree. There is something about them that is not sitting right. I don't know what it is, but they are not being honest with us," Cami said from the back seat.

"Why do you say that?"

"Because she wanted to keep your phone. It was in the way she pulled it away wanting the code."

"I think it was just that she was desperate to call her family and feared it wouldn't work," Theo said hopefully. "I'd hate to think they were up to something with the kids in tow."

"Cami's right, there is something off about the way she spoke when leaving the message. Why say crossing the Mexico border on I-25?"

Joey was tipping the map over and following the highway to Mexico, "Uh guys...?"

"One second," Doug said and turned back to Theo, "It felt like a code the way she emphasized Mexico and I-25."

"Guys," Joey insisted.

Both of them simultaneously said, "What?"

"I was looking at the map and I-25 turns into 1-10."

"Ok highways merge all the time, what about it?"

"Well, If I am looking at this right, I-25 ends at I-10, but neither one of them cross the border into Mexico."

"Let me see that," Cami said, and took the map from him. Her finger traced the highway all the way to the Mexican border and her eyes widened. "He's right."

Her finger traced the map and in two miles the route 50 interchange would lead them to route 285 south. "Ok I think we should take route 50 west. Let's change it up and get off the highway and we won't have to go through Pueblo."

"Sounds good, we can stop a little ways in and see if their demeanor changes."

The exit sign emerged in the distance one quarter mile to go. At the exit the Jeep veered off and followed the road to the new route. The truck followed without hesitation, and they were on their way toward Salida where they would again change direction.

"It should be a couple of hours till we reach the interchange. We could stop for lunch in an obscure area and explain that they will still be on track but that you have a relative in Salina you want to check on," Doug looked at Theo who nodded.

"Perfect, they will want to use the phone, but I'll say even it can't get a signal in that area. We can watch for their reaction and see if their attitude changes. It is possible that she was unaware and wanted someone at the border to get them across."

"Perhaps," Doug said and continued to drive.

An hour later, a small pull off on the side of the road just past Canyon City offered access to the river for the boys to play while providing ample space for the small group. The truck pulled in behind them and Joey fidgeted in his seat wanting to check out the river.

"This is an awesome stop," he exclaimed.

Theo looked around and felt good about the area. The phone would have a signal, but he unlocked it and turned off the service before putting it back into his pocket just in case.

They all exited the Jeep and stretched. Doug waved them over and shooed Joey off with the boys to play in the river. It wasn't deep but he admonished them to be careful on the rocks.

Joey squealed and waved to the boys, "Marcus, Al, c'mon! Let's check it out!"

Gretchen and Mario approached, and he asked, "Why are we stopping?"

"I thought we could use a bite to eat," Cami said.

"Oh, that sounds wonderful," Gretchen smiled, "I am hungry and the boys ate all the snacks."

"Good, I was thinking we could make this our good meal. I doubt we will make Albuquerque today and will likely need to camp someplace."

Gretchen looked at Mario and waved for him to wait a moment. "Can you spin the truck around so we can use the tailgate as a workspace and table?"

"Sure thing," he hopped in and fired it up, doing a three point turn to spin it around and back up to within about five feet of the trailer.

Cami put her hand up for him to stop calling out, "Perfect!"

He hopped out and waved at the girls as he walked past and approached the side of the Jeep where Doug and Theo stood. Mario clapped his hand on Doug's shoulder, "I can't tell you how pleased I was when you pulled off and took this route. After the rest area, I didn't feel good about just cruising down the interstate. Good Call." He nodded.

"We were curious about Gretchen's message to your family; do you think they will meet you?" Theo fished a bit more.

"Honestly, we've never met them. It's a number her mother gave her before she died to seek out her other relatives. We're a little nervous about going there, I'm Italian, not Mexican and she is very American. Her grandparents moved to the U.S. back in the 1960's. Even her mother was born here."

"Then why are you going to Mexico?" Theo asked.

"That's all we could think of. Neither of us have any family here, we don't know what else to do."

Doug and Theo glanced at one another knowingly and walked with Mario toward the river to watch the boys while the ladies prepared a meal. Theo felt at ease and they ate a hearty meal before moving on.

TWENTY-SEVEN

JACE

Tears of joy overwhelmed them all as they swooned over the baby. Amanda produced the bottle and a baggie full of warmed formula from under her arm. Pouring it into the small bottle, she offered it to him, and he suckled hungrily.

"I planned to get him some stuff but didn't find any yet," Kelly protested.

Jace jerked her by the arm and flung her toward the bike. "I always knew you were sneaky and conniving. I knew you trapped me with the baby, and I knew that there was a chance it wasn't mine. I decided long ago to take care of him and that is what I plan to do," he snarled at her.

"Well, we don't need you," she snapped back.

He reached into his satchel and pulled out the small

box, flinging it at her. "I can't believe I was going to ask you to marry me." He spat at the ground in front of her, "It is you *we* don't need, not the other way around." He pointed to Amanda and the baby, "He is my son, and you will get your shit together if you want to be part of his life. The only reason I don't wring your neck right here and now is because you are his mother. Unfortunately for him."

Jace looked her up and down and shoved her toward Rayne in no kind way. "Rayne, can you find her some appropriate riding clothes?"

"Sure." Rayne nodded to Jace, then glared at her. "C'mon, there's a store over there that might have something."

Kelly looked at the store, sporting goods, and grimaced. "You want me to wear something from there?"

"It's either that or we squeeze your fat ass into something I have." She looked at her own clothes. "Which is pretty much what you're gonna find in here. You need to dress practical, and those high heeled shoes are not gonna cut it." She eyed her before turning toward the store. She sighed at her, "Let's go, we need to get a move on."

Kelly trudged off behind Rayne flashing hateful looks back to Jace as she disappeared into the store. One of the guys who'd showed up followed to make sure the girls had a lookout while they shopped, and the others gathered around Amanda and the baby.

"How are we going to do this?" Anthony asked.

"I'm not sure," Jace sighed. "I haven't thought past the idea of getting my son back. We need to get out of here and Rayne's family will be in Albuquerque. This place is FUBAR and it won't be long before we are, too."

The others nodded to him, Boon licked his hand and tucked his head under it, while Amanda and Maria smiled at him and the baby. He absentmindedly reached into his pocket for the small pouch of jerky and offered Boon a snack.

He looked at them wondering when he'd become the guiding force to this rag tag group of survivors, but he had. The baby and his quest for him became a polarizing theme that they all needed to focus on.

Boon licked his hand and whined for more. His eyes fell to those big brown eyes, and he looked back up. "We should eat. Let's find a restaurant we can cook in and find some food. We can map out the direction and gather everyone together and prepare to go."

Amanda and Anthony both nodded to him, showing their support and bolstering his confidence.

One of the guys, an older one, grinned at him. His white beard somewhere about mid chest, he stroked it and glanced around the small circle that was quickly growing with the others. "Sounds good to me and perhaps we can discuss what's in Albuquerque."

The group all had motorcycles, Jace's had a sidecar for Boon and the old man had a trike. These might cause issues if they ran into any spaces that would struggle with the width but they decided to cross that bridge when they came to it. The sidecar could be disconnected and dragged through any smaller gaps by hand but the trike might be more difficult.

They grabbed some maps from their earlier scavenging and laid them out on the tables. Rayne and Kelly walked in with a backpack for her carrying extra clothes and dressed in new sweats and hiking boots. Kelly looked down at herself and sneered in disgust before the guy that was with them shoved her into the small restaurant.

She slumped in a booth at the far end, alone, while the others leaned over a table with the maps. One of the other guys was a short order cook and immediately began to whip up some food while two others gathered anything that was non-perishable. Rayne dragged in two five-gallon water containers she'd found at the sporting goods store and commenced to fill them.

"Where are we going to put them?" Anthony asked.

"I don't know, but I'm sure it is more important than even food that we make sure to have plenty of water."

"She's right," another guy said. "It is a desert with nothing but sand dunes part of the way. We also will need to fill the bikes and keep them full at every broken-down car, stop, or dealership; and grab a couple of gas cans. That sportster with the peanut tank won't make it without a fill up."

The food was amazing and some of the ladies helped

pack up sandwiches and leftovers for the road. Every saddleback and backpack was filled to capacity, the front of the sidecar was stuffed and everyone carried a pack. The bikes without riders on the back were strapped with milk crates full of things or duffels they scavenged from the sporting goods stores. A few small tents and a small cook stove were stowed because the seven hundred miles would not be made in a day. They figured on two to three hundred miles per day.

Jace, Ant, Amanda, Rayne, and Maria sat at one table while the four guys and three women sat at the next one. Kelly sulked at her own table waiting for someone to bring her a plate. No one did, she had to get it for herself. She grumbled as she snatched a plate from the counter and Rayne quietly snickered to Amanda.

Anthony introduced his friends, "That tall wiry guy is Needles."

Rayne cut him off, "Did you say Needles?"

"Well yeah," he laughed. "His name is Chris, but everyone calls him Needles cause he's skinny enough to pass through anything… Kind of like a needle."

Needles stood and bowed. "At your service ladies."

Anthony continued, "Over there is Ray and his Ole' Lady Sheila."

"Ole' lady?" again Rayne interrupted.

Anthony laughed again. "I guess we will have to teach her the terminology, eh guys?" He turned to her and explained, "Wives or girlfriends are called Ole' Ladies. It is a term of honor in a club."

"Oh." Rayne looked embarrassed.

He smiled at her, and Amanda giggled. "You need an Ole' Lady too."

He quickly looked away and finished his introductions. "The old coot is Dennis and the lady beside him is his… *wife,*" he accentuated the words. "Mary. Then the ugly one on the end is Gears," he paused and looked at Rayne, "Gary but we call him Gears because he is always messing with things and inventing shit. He is also the mechanic of the bunch. Next to him is Mora." He turned and whispered to Rayne, "She's not his Ole' Lady but wants to be." He winked at her.

He then asked, "Anyone got a spare brain bucket for the scowling face in the corner?"

"Oh my God can we please speak English," Rayne growled and smacked the table. The others laughed heartily.

"I got one," Needles called out. "Never know when you might bump into a cutie needing a ride." He waggled his eyebrows and winked at her.

She snorted in disgust and looked intently at her food. Jace winked at Amanda who quietly snickered, "We should make her ride with Needles."

His eyebrows raised at that thought because he didn't want her anywhere near him. He was so disgusted with her that the very thought of her touching him right now made him shudder. He nodded and leaned into Anthony. "You think Needles will let her ride with him?"

"I'd say that is a hard yep but will ask him to be sure. Sure would be great to watch her face when we tell her where she's riding after the look she gave him."

"Thanks."

Jace and the others rose and went outside to prepare to leave. Kelly of course cringed when Needles wrapped his arm around her saying, "Looks like you're with me, little lady."

Jace and Anthony looked at one another while Amanda tucked Baby Jason into a Boba Wrap baby sling, wrapped tight to her body.

No matter what they said to Kelly to encourage her to breastfeed the infant, she refused. They prepared bags of formula that different people would tuck into underarms or waistbands to keep warm for when it came time to feed him. Boon hopped playfully into his sidecar grunting at the stuff that was taking up part of his seat and shimmying it aside to get settled.

The roar echoed off of the buildings as they pulled out and headed for the highway. Deciding to avoid Phoenix, they headed for the fifteen to the forty and west from there right into Albuquerque. With the sun high overhead, they hoped to get out of L.A. before sunset and they felt sure that this would be the most treacherous leg of their journey.

Anthony took the front door to their little group of riders while Dennis picked up the back as they headed out. Two by two they rode through the deserted streets, Kelly's shrill voice carried on the wind with complaints of all kinds, but no one heard or cared. The wind in their faces and city at their backs was the only thing they cared about.

Onto the ten and toward the mountains Jace was so fond of; they rode, weaving between the cars lined on the roadway with ease. Jace looked back at the city from an overpass and was glad to see it go.

Thank you for reading. Please consider leaving a review.

Continue the story

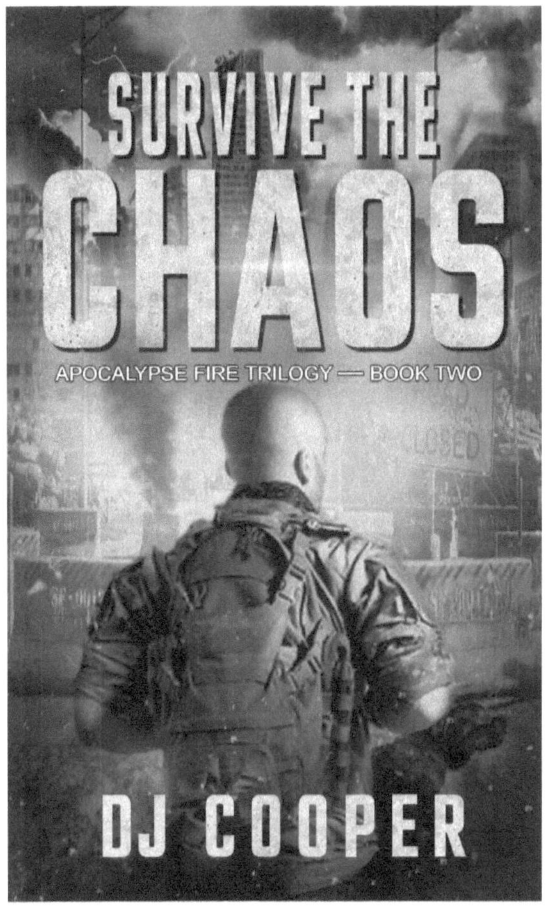

Book 2 of the Apocalypse Fire Trilogy

https://www.amazon.com/dp/B09QQSQ837

ABOUT THE AUTHOR

DJ Cooper is the Bestselling author of the apocalypse.

She tells a funny story about driving a truck and says, "It all started with the Dystopia series." Released in late 2014 it fueled her desire to not only write stories but to help others on the path to preparedness.

A strong desire to learn more led her back to school in hopes of gaining more perspective on the craft and the industry. She holds a Bachelor of Arts in English, a Master of Science in Marketing, and is currently, a student at Southern New Hampshire University studying for her Master of Fine Arts in English/Creative writing with a concentration in teaching. She studied Graphic Design and designs book covers as well through Dauntless Cover Design.

Writing the apocalypse is a passion and as a prominent figure in the preparedness community with Prepper Podcast Radio, the Self-Reliant Expo, she works to bring knowledge of preparedness and sustainable living through varied forms of media.

Find out more at https://authoroftheapocalypse.com

Contact the Author https://linktr.ee/AuthorDJCooper

Join our reader groups on Facebook

https://www.facebook.com/groups/writtenapocalypse

Follow me:

https://www.facebook.com/AuthorDJCooper

Https://twitter.com/djcooper2015

https://www.tiktok.com/@authordjcooper

And don't forget to sign up for the newsletter

https://bit.ly/3KmAGjh